HEALERS OF THE NIGHT

Young intern Sheila Devaney finds more
than enough drama to be had each night in
Casualty, without the added excitement of
finding that her senior house-surgeon
Mark Leighton is the man she almost
married five years earlier ... Neither has
married anyone else, although Mark
appears to be considerably attracted to one
of his female colleagues. But does trying to
put the clock back ever work?

HEALERS OF THE NIGHT

Anne Vinton

ATLANTIC LARGE PRINT
Chivers Press, Bath, England.
John Curley & Associates Inc.,
South Yarmouth, Mass., USA.

Fic
VIN
Large
Print

Library of Congress Cataloging in Publication Data

Vinton, Anne.
 Healers of the night.

 (Atlantic large print)
 Originally published: London : Mills & Boon, 1968.
 1. Large type books. I. Title
 [PR6072.I54H43 1987]   823'.914   87–15462
 ISBN 1–55504–465–4 (pbk.)

British Library Cataloguing in Publication Data

Vinton, Anne
 Healers of the night.—(Atlantic large
 print).
 I. Title
 823'.914 [F]   PR6072.I54

 ISBN 0–7451–9288–2

This Large Print edition is published by Chivers Press, England, and
John Curley & Associates, Inc, U.S.A. 1987

Published by arrangement with Harlequin Enterprises B.V.

U.K. Hardback ISBN 0 7451 9288 2
U.S.A. Softback ISBN 1 55504 465 4

HEALERS OF THE NIGHT

CHAPTER ONE

The deep purple nimbus cloud, streaked at its core with ash-grey, hung like a miasma over the city and down poured the thunder rain, in sheets, emptying the street of pedestrians. Public houses, now open, filled quickly with irregulars who could make a half-pint of beer last the duration of the storm; in all enclosed places there was the smell of steam from wet macs and hair. The storm had threatened all day, making the air close and sultry: most people were relieved it had broken at last; gardeners were glad of the downpour. There were those pessimists who foretold, 'This will break up the good weather. You'll see. We've had our usual three weeks of summer. All we can expect in this damned climate.'

In only one place in the whole of the sprawling city were the elements unimportant, in fact scarcely noticed. This was within that tightly enclosed world, the general hospital of St John. Attached to the university, the Medical School block linking the hospital proper with the new Medical Sciences wing, donated by a local self-made millionaire who had been saved from an early death by that modern wonder the kidney machine, the hospital and its adjuncts were only concerned with getting on with the job, hoping to get done in time but each individual fretting that he or she never would. There was always so much to do and too few to do it. Plenty of medical students, of course, some of whom would never finish the course. These usually gained their practical knowledge by getting in everybody else's way. The nurses were usually more adept at doing dressings and the parading consultants were inclined to hang on to their knowledge as though it was a State secret. Occasionally they spoke ventriloquist-wise to their attending registrars, but the bunch of students at the tail end of the procession had to be versed in lip-reading to be any the wiser.

At this hour of day, while the thunder ripped and roared outside, wanting ten minutes to the half-hour after seven, the hospital was thick with earnest-looking students, who, having finished their normal stint for the day, were seeking practical knowledge wherever they could. Mostly they worked in twos, but there were lone wolves, too, who were either dedicated doctors in the making or big-heads anxious not to share their findings with their fellows. They hung anxiously around in the corridors outside the closed wards, where the bed-pan round was being performed, waiting for visitors to be admitted. When it became obvious that some patients were being neglected by either family or friends, that they, in fact, could look forward to an hour of sheer boredom, then the students advanced, drew screens and provided entertainment for the duration, with Sister's full permission, of course. It was entertaining to be observed, palpated and auscultated in the chest and abdomen when one was hospitalised with an affliction of the foot, for instance. Sister must have known, also, that the questionnaire part of the student examinations provided script material for cross-talk comedians. Patients were also people, many of whom had a sense of humour as sharp as a lancet.

As the visitors, dripping all over the shining hospital corridors, advanced, so the professionals, that is the trained medical staff and most of the nurses, went in the direction of the various dining-rooms. For the doctors it was dinner, but the nurses dined at midday and called the evening meal supper. It was usually the same menu in both camps.

In one of the medical wards Sister Briggs had a word with one of her favourite young medicos, a woman with honey-blonde hair and grey eyes which belied her Irish ancestry. She had been setting up a saline drip and the patient was anxious to see her visitors while the novelty of her condition was still upon her.

'I had a haemorrhage after tea,' she greeted her wan-looking husband and fuzzy-haired mother. 'Now look at me!'

Sheila Devaney smiled at Sister.

'The times I've done that!' she exclaimed. 'But I suppose if you're the patient it *is* quite an event. Would you know what the food's like this evening, Sister?'

'No. Somebody said Outpatients was redolent of fried onions, and that's nearest the kitchens. Could be liver or, with a bit of luck, pork chops. I believe you're changing duty, Doctor?'

'Yes. I'm on night casualty for a week, starting tonight.'

'Poor you! Would you believe it if it wasn't happening to you personally? How do they expect you to cope when you're just going off day duty at half-past seven?'

'Well, it's my first night duty since I came here, so I can't grumble yet. I shall bolt my food and lie down for an hour, and—who knows? maybe we'll have a quiet night.'

'You must be joking, Doctor! I was nursing in this hospital before there was a University and a medical school, if you can imagine anybody sticking it so long, and even then you could be sure of excitement in Casualty every night. You can't imagine what people get up to once it's dark.'

'Sister!'

'Now, Doctor, you know what I mean. Well, I hope you survive the week.'

They went their ways. Sheila looked round the junior dining-room for a quiet spot where she could eat and dash off a note to Bruce at the same time. Bruce was her fiancé, a doctor in general practice, and fifteen years her senior. She was almost twenty-five and occupied with her year's internship at St John's. Once this was completed, in nine months' time, she intended getting married and joining Bruce in practice in the pleasant south-coastal town where he lived and worked. It was a safe, pleasant prospect, and it was this which helped her to regard a twenty-four-hour stretch of duty with equanimity.

Of course it was impossible to write very personally with a hundred and fifty young men and women chattering and laughing fifty to the dozen. The main course was sausages with fried onions and at the next table two young men were holding a forensic discussion on the contents of a sausage. On the other side a young Indian gentleman was saying, 'It breathes and blinks and reacts to an injection. I saw it with my own eyes. If it had got up

5

from the table and walked I wouldn't have been surprised. You can kill it and resuscitate it, also. All done with computers.'

'They'll have babies by computers next,' drawled a lazy English voice. 'A woman will decide to have a child when it suits her, say in December when it's cool, so she'll be suitably programmed, artificially inseminated and automatically conceive in March. Then—bingo!'

'I suppose by "bingo" you mean she then proceeds to have her child naturally?' inquired a female voice.

'Of course. She wouldn't know she'd had it, otherwise.'

'What do you mean by "of course". If you're using computers to take the pleasure out of childbearing you might as well take the pain out, too. It's just like men to invent computers for their own convenience without considering women at all.'

A few young men began to chant, banging the tables for accompaniment: 'Chain yourself to the railings, Emily, or they won't give you the vote ...' Before this could get out of hand, however, the dining-room supervisor came over and suggested that the singers might like to eat or leave the room, as others were waiting to come in.

Sheila wrote, while eating with her left

hand, 'We've just had a minor sex war in the dining-room. They're always breaking out. I do think that unattached women can be terribly touchy and I'm so glad that I *am* attached to you. Dear old you . . .' She almost crossed out 'old', remembering that age-gap of fifteen years and the way Bruce was inclined to dwell on it at times, but this would look rather obvious and she had to get a letter off to Bruce this evening even though it only said 'hello' and 'goodbye' . . . 'I'm going on a night stint,' she continued, 'in Casualty. As you know, darling, this is a big city and I'm led to believe I can expect the night life to be fairly hectic. There are two of us on call, one medical (me) and one surgical. I don't know anybody on the surgical side, only a very glamorous woman who wears a sari. It's possible not to know anybody really well in such a vast place, not that I really want to, knowing that I have you. I was going to take a walk and fill my lungs, but I hear it's raining, so I'll lie down for an hour and try to sleep. Have a lovely week's fishing, darling, and if you're to get this before you leave for North Devon I must catch the post stat. All my love . . .'

Reading the missive through, Sheila thought, 'Not exactly passionate, is it? Well, Bruce will understand that continuous duty

7

doesn't exactly make for passion. In any case I don't think Bruce and I are exactly torrid lovers. We're comfortable, rather. I think it's far more satisfying to be on a comfortable level with somebody rather than up on peaks of ecstasy one minute and down in hell the next.' She frowned at her thoughts for a moment, vaguely disturbed. 'In any case,' she told herself sharply, 'I was very young at the time and I got all that nonsense out of my system.'

*　　*　　*

Sir William Bender was entertaining two members of St John's staff to dinner. They were also members of his team—his speciality was thoracic surgery—and they were Martha Haley, his registrar, and Mark Leighton, the senior house-surgeon. The situation as Sir William saw it was that Martha had fallen a little for Mark without the reverse, as yet, being obvious. It was to encourage young Leighton to use his eyes as nature intended, regarding a beautiful woman at leisure, that Sir William had asked him to his table.

Martha was beautiful as a sculpture is beautiful; her hair was black and plentiful, smoothly coiffured and shining; her eyes were emeralds, faintly aslant, and her studied smile never quite reached them.

Though they were about the same age—Mark was thirty-two—he had never thought about Martha outside the context of their working together. She was streets ahead of him professionally, in any case, and a man rarely looks on an upper shelf for his mate. It is his prerogative to elevate, if anything. In any case Mark was concerned with his career; he was older than the average house-surgeon and couldn't see beyond the thesis for his MD diploma at the moment. He was enjoying his dinner but otherwise not exactly playing up as expected.

'Martha tells me you're doing a week's stint on Casualty?' the host demanded bluffly. 'What a lot of damned nonsense. I shall ask Admin what the hell they're playing at!'

'Oh, I don't mind, sir,' Mark said hastily. 'It's all grist to the mill.'

'But you're not a potty little general surgeon. You're a chest man. Anybody can stitch up a drunk who's been bashed over the head with a bottle. And in any case I mind anybody messing a member of my team about. Martha minds, don't you, my dear?'

'Oh, Sir William, *I* don't run the hospital.'

'Shall we ask for him to be let off?'

'No, please, sir,' Mark spoke for himself, 'if you don't mind. I'm only standing by for the usual week and I'll be glad of the afternoons to

9

complete my thesis. It might turn out a very valuable week to me.'

'Keen as mustard, that's the way I like 'em,' boomed Sir William. 'I remember writing my thesis on paroxysmal myocardia. I didn't know a damned thing about it, but I was very good at assimilating facts and setting them down. When a heart man offered me a job on the strength of my success I simply had to start taking the subject seriously, and surgery came much later. I don't think I should really have told you that or you may decide to change your minds and run over to the medical side. How about some brandy and coffee now, eh?'

Mark said he really ought to be leaving, however.

'I'm on duty tonight, sir, and it's after nine already.'

'If I may point out, Leighton, there are advantages in senior appointments. One usually gets a night's rest in bed.'

'I shall hope to follow your example in due course, sir. Meanwhile, thanks for your hospitality.'

'I'll go back with you, Mark,' Martha suggested.

'That's right,' encouraged Sir William, 'hold hands in the Tube.'

Mark smiled, thinking this to be a joke, but

Martha's eyes were lowered and he fancied she might be offended at the idea of holding hands with a mere house-surgeon. He had learnt in the short time he had been at St John's to respect the registrar of such an eminent man as Sir William; she was obviously hand-picked. He was courtesy itself on the way back, but did not presume on the recent occasion to force familiarity between them. It was she who made a suggestion for a further meeting as they walked through the grounds of the University buildings to the back entrance of the hospital where the residential building was situated.

'Mark, don't work on your wretched thesis every day. I'm off on Wednesday afternoon and I'd like you to come and help me buy a car, a good second-hand one I have my eye on. One appreciates a man's help at such times.'

'Well, Martha, I'm no mechanic . . .'

'I'm sure you're better than I am. I don't even know what a big end is. I'll meet you at the gate at three, then?'

'If I'm your man, very well, Martha. I'm sure you could do better, though.'

'Now don't be modest, Mark.' Her green eyes swept him briefly before she turned on her high heels to go to her room in Women's Residence. He would do very well indeed for all her needs, she decided, and she had waited a long time to meet him. She was not without experience with men; she had the sort of face and figure which demanded an escort; but she had always known that it would take a great deal in any one man to satisfy her, and Mark Leighton was the likeliest candidate for her favours to date.

*   *   *

The Senior Casualty Officer turned with a sigh as Sheila Devaney reported for duty.

'You're early, thank God,' he said brusquely. 'I don't want to see another plaster pail for a week. Four ankle fractures during the past hour while I've been on my own! This is Staff Nurse Collins, by the way, who will do most of the work for you if you keep on the right side of her, and Nurse Lewis, the junior. Nurse makes the best coffee; Staff isn't at all domesticated.'

'Now, Doctor, that's my reputation you're maligning,' the West Indian staff nurse said in her musical, calypso voice. 'You'd better go off duty while you're in one piece. Nurse Lewis, make one of your famous cuppas while I show Doctor round. It's your first night duty, isn't it, Doctor?'

'Yes, Staff, and I'm terrified.'

'Oh, don't be. We manage one way and

another. Oh, there's this lot to deal with.' She indicated a group of students somewhat contemptuously.

'Are they all ill?' asked Sheila innocently.

'Oh, lawd, I wouldn't know. Probably, by the looks of them. But for our purposes they're volunteers for night duty. You're supposed to choose three and send the others off to bed.'

'Oh. Well, you and you and you,' Sheila decided, wondering at the deep gulf which separated the student of a year ago from the doctor of today. She couldn't imagine herself looking so young and eager and naïve, somehow, as the three who immediately assumed importance in front of their rejected fellows. They were set to work filling drums with dressings, making swabs and generally remedying the deficiencies created by a normal day. Sheila met Bill, the night porter, who had a cubbyhole off the Outpatients' Hall and, according to the staff nurse, was given to taking liberties with female staff.

'Never turn your back on him, Doctor, or you'll be black and blue where you sit down tomorrow.'

There was the ambulance team who manned the white vehicle standing at the ready outside the emergency entrance—Jock and Phil, laughingly referred to by the staff nurse as 'Jack and Jill'. She asked after Jock's family; he had five children.

'Mary wasn't home when I left,' he said, 'and her mother was saying she'd get a belting when she did show up. Gone to the pictures with one of her pals and then you know how it is, stopping here and chatting there instead of getting on home?'

'Mary's the eldest, she's nine,' explained the West Indian. 'He's a devoted family man, is Jock. He'll be showing you all his snapshots before the night's out.'

After meeting the night orderly, a crinkly-haired young Italian, Sheila asked, 'Isn't there somebody missing? I'm not on my own tonight, am I?'

'I shouldn't think so, Doctor. Mr Ritchie was to have been on with you, but I heard he'd fallen during a tennis match and got a Potts' fracture. I have no idea who's coming in his place.'

There was the sound of hurrying footsteps through the empty Outpatients' Hall and Mark Leighton appeared with a general nod to all concerned.

'Good evening, everybody. Sorry I'm late, but I had a stitch-abscess sprung on me. Are we busy?'

'No, Mr Leighton,' said the staff nurse. 'I have nothing for you at the moment.'

Mark's glance raked Sheila briefly and ricocheted back.

'Long time no see,' he remarked.

'It's a very long time,' she agreed, feeling as though she was choking.

The silence that followed was awkward and seemed interminably long.

'Well, who has forty winks?' asked Mark, indicating the room down the corridor where Casualty Officers could try to sleep between events if they so wished. 'It should be ladies first.'

'No, no,' she said quickly, 'I'm not at all tired. You go and have a nap.'

'Very well.' He looked at the nurse, but he spoke to her in six significant words. 'Call me if you need me,' he said.

CHAPTER TWO

Sheila was glad of that quiet first hour when all she had to do was lance a carbuncle situated in a very awkward place for comfort.

The Irish navvy straightened up ruefully, his native humour returning now that the pain was eased.

'That's the first time I've dropped my pants so eagerly,' he joked. 'The last time my schoolteacher gave me a dozen of the best.'

'I'm sure you deserved every stroke,' Sheila told him, as she entered up the dosage of penicillin she had given him in the log-book.

The lugubrious Nurse Lewis, quietly droll, thrust yet another cup of coffee at the young doctor.

'You'll need this,' she said confidently, 'to keep you awake for a bit. After closing time you won't need to try to fight nature. I'm going to cast on the second sleeve of my cardigan living in hopes that I'll ever wear the thing. Night duty in Cas is very wearing. I feel every bit of twenty-two at the moment.'

'You poor old thing,' Sheila sympathised. She sat on the edge of one of the examination couches and pondered on that surprise meeting with Mark after five long years. It proved the vastness of St John's that they were both working in the hospital and had never crossed paths previously. It must be some quirk of fate that had put them on duty together, like this, and Mark had been as startled to see her as she him. For a moment there had been a curtain rent between them and she had remembered him as he had been, offended, hurt and resolutely walking away from her towards his own future, tugging her heartstrings with him. From that day to this she hadn't set eyes on him, and all her

16

assiduous enquiries, at first desperate and later merely curious, had proved fruitless.

Sheila had been in her second year at medical school when she had first become aware of the handsome medic in his final year who had many of the women students in absolute twitters. Sheila attended the New Year dance with Mark, and when he didn't attempt to kiss her she was painfully disappointed. Things progressed from that point, however, so that when they did kiss they were deeply in love, apparently hopelessly. When Mark qualified, leaving Sheila with four more years of study ahead of her, the affair seemed impossible. Mark had suggested an engagement, but Sheila, who was in love for the first time in her life, wanted only to be a wife, and yet knew she must carry on with the career for which she had already fought her widowed, despotic mother, who thought it was the plain duty of all daughters to do as they were advised by their elders. Funnily enough it was Mrs Devaney who had put forward the very argument which then troubled Sheila. 'Doctoring's all right for a man, but those six years are important in a woman's life in other ways. That's the time she meets young men and usually decides to get married. Putting such things off might mean she never marries at all, and if you're going to say "So what?" I would remind you of Jenny Forster.' The legend of Jenny was that she had been a beautiful girl, the belle of the village where Sheila and her mother had lived after Major Devaney's death. All the young men chased after Jenny, but she was a modern young thing with ideas of her own and was outspoken about marriage hampering a girl's other prospects. Sheila, then eight, had admired the eighteen-year-old Jenny as a goddess endowed with all natural attributes. When Sheila came home finally from boarding school, ten years later, Jenny looked a little shrunken, her cheeks pinched, her eyes larger and somehow wary and—most significant of all—the young men who had been her contemporaries were now either married to other girls or gone away and Jenny's solitary companion was a neurotic-looking pug on a leash. According to Mrs Devaney, Jenny had suffered three nervous breakdowns during the past year and was at present in the grip of a phobia which prevented her leaving the narrow confines of the village where she had lived all her life.

'If she'd married, and not had such stupid ideas about freedom for girls, she would be a different woman today,' Mrs Devaney had said flatly, 'and I don't want my only daughter turning out like Jenny Forster.'

Torn between the idea of becoming like Jenny, a victim of frustrations, and giving up the career which was half her life's blood, Sheila became unsettled and sharp-tongued. She picked a quarrel with Mark, though they made up almost immediately and laughed about it. Next day it became easier to quarrel again, however, and this time the making up was delayed.

'Look!' Mark had said. 'Are we going on together, Sheila, or not? Make up your mind. I have a train to catch at nine.'

'Oh, you must catch your train, of course,' a demon spoke through Sheila's lips. 'Nothing else is quite so important.'

'Do you think we might be making a mistake?'

'The whole damned business has been a mistake, if you ask me. You are *Doctor* Leighton now, and you're obviously wasting your time with small fry like me.'

'Am I wasting my time?' he had asked seriously, his eyes dark and intense upon hers.

'Well, I've hardly seen you for a week and then you ask me to get engaged! I think engagements are stupid between people who are going to be separated. One is better to be free.' She had felt rather like a disciple of Jenny's as she had said this. Absolute freedom was often the heaviest fetter in the world, if, as well as being free, one was alone.

He had said in a stranger's voice, 'Very well, Sheila. All the best. I'm sorry to be a bore, but I have to get my train.' He had raised his hand once in salute and turned and walked away. Something in her had screamed out, as he went, which she afterwards described as sheer panic. She had been dreadfully unhappy and recovered, as one does, when there is work to be done and the vacuum caused can be filled by many things. Also she had been in and out of love again, not finding it as devastating an experience the second time, and now there was Bruce, kind, solid, dependable and predictable. She was lucky to have met someone like Bruce of whom her mother entirely approved, thinking her daughter had been clever to gain for herself the best of both worlds, a career and a fiancé with such qualities.

Seeing Mark again, however, had been rather upsetting. She had sometimes imagined such a meeting and she had always seen herself being self-possessed, casual and unemotional, saying such things as 'Well, how nice to see you again! What's happened to you these past years? Really? I must be off now, but it's been so pleasant hearing your news.' Instead there had been that unexpected inner rending and moments of inarticulate

20

emotional confusion, and then, her larynx still expanded, her response of 'It is a very long time,' every word heavy with regret.

'This is stupid,' she now chivvied herself. 'We had our little affair, but we both knew it was hopeless from the start. We should have made the break much earlier than we did. I was often very unhappy with Mark, whereas Bruce would die rather than upset me. There's the difference.'

But the unhappiness was a two-edged thing and sometimes she had hurt Mark, she knew, with a sort of perverted revelling in a power which could not find its true expression owing to their circumstances. He was the one who had been quite casual over their unexpected reunion, as was proved by his being able to go away and sleep. She wouldn't be able to sleep this night, she knew, not until she had discovered whether he was married or not, and what had befallen him during these past five years.

*   *   *

The plot for the first drama of the hospital night was already set and relentlessly unfolding towards it climax. In the suburb of Brombury stood a block of luxury flats occupying an eminence overlooking the park and, beyond that, the river. The rich lived here, for rentals were high, and the cars were sleek and high-powered, matching the individuals who drove them. Most of the flats were lit at this hour, half-past ten on a June evening. The earlier storm had drifted away west and the air was purer and cleaner than it had been for days, with smells of wet earth, refreshed grass and dashed roses.

The night porter and lift boy at Park Mansions enjoyed the first cuppa of their spell of duty together in the comfortable basement.

'Anything exciting ever happen here, George?' the boy asked the older man. 'Lift get stuck for hours, for instance?'

'Nothing like that, son,' George replied. 'Too new and well-oiled. If some of these folk had to walk upstairs there'd be questions asked about it in Parliament. Got some MPs here, y'know. One old boy had a stroke in a toilet once. That was quite a do. We couldn't get at 'im. Rigor mortis had set in and we 'ad to take the door off the 'inges.'

'I wish something would 'appen tonight. I'm bored.'

'Now don't you go asking for trouble, young feller-me-lad. This is your first time on nights and I don't want you tampering with the lift nor nothing of that nature. Read your comic, or whatever you young lads do read

22

nowadays, and be prepared to take the residents home when they come back from the theatre and nightclubs. They don't want to get stuck—they just want to sleep it off at that time of night. Then you can 'ave a nap if you're a good lad and it'll be morning in no time.'

The phone rang shrilly behind him.

'Nah what?' asked George. 'This is the outside line, too. Yes?' he put on his most refined accent as he lifted the receiver. 'Park Mansions—porter here.'

'George? This is Esher—Gerald Esher.'

'Yes, Mr Esher, sir? What can I do for you?'

'I was supposed to be home to dinner, but something came up and I got involved. I may be late back and I can't get a reply to my number.'

'I haven't seen Mrs Esher go out, sir. Of course—'

'No, she hasn't wanted to go out lately. Not been too well. I wonder if you would give her a call and make sure she's all right? I'm at the Bar Club, and please tell my wife I expect to be back just after midnight...' Gerald Esher hesitated to add, 'Give her my love.' He wanted to, but one didn't involve house porters in that sort of domestic twaddle. He had meant to be home to dinner,

23

remembering Elaine's somewhat hysterical outburst over breakfast that morning, her embarrassed, panic-stricken accusation that he was seeing another woman.

'For a long time now,' she had insisted, keeping her voice down as they had learnt to do, because with the veranda windows open sounds carried to the other flats, 'you've been seeing another woman, I know.'

'Elaine dear, you're overwrought. Now don't be silly.'

'Then why haven't you dined at home one single night this week? Am I a leper? I sit alone night after night like a recluse.'

A long, forbearing masculine sigh had been the only response. Gerald Esher did not believe in wordy quarrels with his wife. They had always been above that sort of thing.

'I suppose she's young and pretty?' Elaine had proceeded. 'They usually are.'

'Elaine, what young, pretty girl would look at me? I'm a dull, fifty-year-old law man, and no Don Juan in looks, either.'

'I notice you don't deny wanting another woman. Well, where—?'

'Elaine, I have to go now. I'm in Court today. I'll be home to dinner unless something important crops up, and we'll have a nice long chat together. I'll let you know if I can't make it. OK?'

Gerald didn't take Elaine's gibing too seriously. He didn't know an awful lot about women even after twenty-five years of marriage and put anything odd down to their sex.

He loved his job, thank God, and it was an escape. Meanwhile he felt uneasy that a new facet of her complaint seemed to be a determination not to answer the phone. He should have rung earlier, he knew, but old Browne had cornered him and kept him nattering about 'The Crown versus Kingsmill' for what seemed like hours. He purposely didn't phone between nine and ten because Elaine liked a long, leisurely bath at this time, without interruptions. When there was no reply at half-past ten he half wondered if she could have fallen asleep in her bath or had some sort of attack. He was glad when old George promised to use his pass-key to enter the apartment should Madam not answer the door. He felt so relieved he strolled back to his companions and ordered another brandy. He liked man-talk, the brown leather atmosphere of the club and the fug of good cigars. Now if Elaine had accosted him with preferring the club to her company then he would have made a straight plea of guilty.

George said, 'Hey, young feller-me-lad, take me up to the third floor and wait. I got to see if the Eshers' phone is out of order or whatever.'

'Can't you take yourself up?'

'I could, if I felt like it, but you're the organ-grinder's monkey, so come on.'

Elaine Esher had had a bad day. Her head had ached ever since that senseless row with Gerald, or rather, non-row, because he refused to fight her. She knew in her heart of hearts that there was no other woman, there was no woman at all in his life, not even her. Another woman was easy to conjure up, young, pretty and desirable because one no longer felt one was any of these things. Having started one had to keep on; the other woman lived with them, always ready to pop up. Gerald was the only one who could cast her out if he chose to do so, but instead of blazing with resentment he would say, 'There, there!' or 'Don't be silly, dear,' and made her edgier and sillier than before.

Today the 'other woman', the shapeless nothing which Gerald preferred to her, was more real than ever. She felt that if she didn't find it, wrestle with it and dispose of it, it would be the end of her. She dreaded facing the end of herself; somehow life had been discovery, or rather a voyage of discovery which hadn't quite got her anywhere; it hadn't brought her the incomparable adventure of motherhood, its fulfilments and trials. She didn't even know if this was her fault or Gerald's, but was inclined to blame herself. She was trapped in the doldrums of her middle-aged existence without prospect of a landfall. Instead of screaming for help her cries came out as wild accusation and experienced nagging over which she seemed to have little control. When Gerald said mildly, 'Why don't you see a doctor, dear?' she turned on him blind with fury. She wasn't ill, she was sick and tired of the nothing she could see stretching ahead of her, the void of the uncharted waters of loneliness which became lonelier with each passing day as Gerald became more and more immersed in his affair with the other woman.

He had promised to come home to dinner this evening. Well, they had better have a long-overdue talk and decide what was to be done, because she didn't like the person she was becoming at all. She did it to drive Gerald to distraction so that he would hit her or something, but Gerald and his 'there, theres' were driving her crazy. She would put on a pretty dress, low-cut, and surprise Gerald with her still-slim figure. She knew, however, that Gerald would blush even at the sight of his own wife's bosom and resolutely look away thereafter, so that she felt indecent and cheap.

Anyway, she would cook something nice; chicken curry. He liked chicken curry better than anything and she hadn't made it for simply ages.

After shopping she began to prepare the meal, but it surprised her how her enthusiasm for the venture had suddenly waned. She didn't want to cook for Gerald at all. The onions burned and she abandoned the idea, leaving the sink full of dirty dishes. She lowered the venetian blinds in the bedroom and lay down for an hour, wondering how long she could make the washing-up last while she was waiting for Gerald. They would go out for a meal—it was ages since they had done that together—then all she would have to do would be to make herself look attractive and dress up.

She told herself quite calmly, when Gerald was half an hour late, that if he didn't come then she would kill herself. The kitchen was cleared and spotless—she had managed to make the task last an hour and a half—she was dressed in a black and silver dress and had piled her hair high on her head. Sitting in front of the mirror she had seen her wrinkles, however, and, never having been a pretty woman, thought she looked old and ugly with a complexion like a suet pudding.

Gerald was an hour late when a car

screeched in the driveway below.

'I'll scare him to death,' she thought. 'He can't do this to me!'

In the bathroom she found Gerald's old cut-throat razor.

'He'll be in the lift now,' Elaine mused, 'so if I cut there'll be blood but no real danger. Where—where does one cut to bleed a lot?'

She had found the artery in her left wrist when the telephone shrilled in the hall. Nobody ever rang her except Gerald, and he was on his way up, wasn't he? She had heard his car. Or was it his car?

Fear washed over her as she watched her blood leaving her body in rhythmic spurts, tried to walk to the telephone, but found her senses leaving her.

'Oh, Gerald!' was her final thought before she lost consciousness, 'what am I doing to you who have always been so kind?'

George's war medals jangled on his chest as he smoothed himself down before knocking on the door of number sixteen, the Eshers' flat. He liked to look his best when calling on his tenants, as he thought of them. His moustache was waxed and his hair sleekly smoothed over his bald patch. He even relaxed his features into a deprecatory smile as he tapped on the door, lightly at first. When he had rung the bell twice and knocked really hard a few times he saw the lad peering at him from the lift-shaft.

'I gotta go down,' said the boy, 'somebody's ringing. You ready yet?'

'No. You go down and come back again when you've finished.'

George fished out his pass-key whistling under his breath and slotted it into the keyhole. He hoped Mrs Esher wasn't in bed and a sound sleeper; she might wake up and think—but he was doing this on Mr Esher's instructions, and that cleared him of any question of intent, not that madam was the sort if you did feel that way inclined. She was a funny lady, avoiding your eye if she could and always making a dart either for the main door or the stairs. George had only clapped eyes on her a couple of times, being night porter. Once she had been running out to post a letter and another time she had been coming in when he arrived on duty, soaked through and looking sort of queer, as though she liked the rain.

He coughed as he entered the hall of the flat and switched on a light.

'Madam, are you there?' he called. After a moment he added, 'Your phone has been ringing and there was no answer.'

George didn't think he was at all psychic, but he had decidedly cold feet about advancing any further. He was a man who did his duty, however, and so he went towards the bedroom, switching lights on as he did so. When he reached the bathroom he gave a small start which was not so much surprise as confirmation. His waxed moustache quivered with emotion.

'Oh, my gawd!' was his reaction.

The phone wasn't out of order, George discovered, which was the one good thing about the whole business.

CHAPTER THREE

Sheila knocked on the door behind which Mark Leighton was, presumably, sleeping, opened it a fraction and said, 'I want you, stat!'

Mark was at her shoulder in an instant, dragging on his white coat.

'What's up?'

Sheila indicated one of the cubicles where a student was keeping a decidedly nervous vigil. Outside in the corridor a constable waited ominously.

'It looks like attempted suicide,' Sheila said. 'Nurse is getting the saline to start a drip going. I've also sent a specimen of blood for

31

cross-matching, but I think we should start her on group "O". She's deeply cyanosed.'

Mark had dismissed the student with a gesture of his thumb. He now sought the pulse on the uninjured side.

'Attempted suicide?' he questioned. 'I would say she damn near succeeded. Any details?'

'No. There's a man who knows her outside; he found her like this. He's a night porter at a block of flats near the park. I thought the first thing was to set up a drip. Will you do it?'

'I think I'd better.' He found time to smile wryly. 'You had no gift for surgery, if I remember rightly?'

'That's a long time ago,' she reminded him. 'I improved as I went along.'

'You mean surgically, of course?'

To this she didn't respond. She uncovered the sterile tray of surgical instruments and watched him cut down to a vein as shrunken as a withered stalk.

The staff nurse pushed through the curtains with a metal stand and a vacolitre of saline.

'She's ABMN and we only have two pints in the Lab,' she announced. 'How many will you need, sir?'

'Four at least,' Mark almost snapped. 'Tell the Lab to get it somehow. Why can't we all have the same blood in our veins?' he growled

32

as Nurse Collins disappeared with a swish of a starched apron.

The saline was fed into the vein while the blood was reaching the required temperature for the infusion.

'As a point of interest,' Sheila volunteered, '*I* am ABMN, too.'

'I didn't know that. Thank God!' he said, after glancing at her speculatively. She didn't know whether it was thank God because it might have worried him, or thank God that he hadn't married her. 'I may have to borrow a pint before morning,' he told her. 'I know doctors are sacrosanct as a rule, but if you will have a rare blood-group you must expect to be tapped when required.'

Looking down at the livid countenance of their patient, Sheila said, 'She can have my blood and welcome if it's needed.'

'Tell one of the lads to come back and watch her. One who can recognise death when he sees it. I somehow don't think he'll have a long wait. We'd better go and get some details about this mess.'

A spark of life still lingered as fresh blood began to drip into Elaine Esher's veins. Gerald Esher arrived looking almost as pallid as his wife, the vaunted reserve of all Englishmen stripped from him, leaving his emotions bare and crumpling his suave countenance into

33

ugliness.

'Doctor, is my wife...?'

'Now, Mr Esher, she's hanging on. If she can survive this first hour every one is one to us thereafter.'

Mark was nice to people, other people, Sheila decided. He really did care about that woman and whatever had driven her to—

'I'm afraid you'll have to talk to the policeman,' Mark was saying softly. 'This business has to be cleared up.'

'I'm sure it was only an accident,' Gerald said quickly. 'My wife was playing about with my razor and it slipped. She—' He looked up and his face crumpled afresh. 'No, it won't wash, will it? I said I'd be home and then I couldn't make it. Elaine hadn't been well. I should have been with her.'

When Mrs Esher had been taken up to a ward, Sheila looked at her colleague, with a small glimmer of self-consciousness.

'Do you want to lie down again? Honestly, I'm not tired.'

'Good! Let's settle down and have a natter for five minutes. If we can have some decent black coffee...?'

Nurse Lewis grumbled, 'I should have worked in a café. Same job, more money, I need my head examining; but the psychiatrist would probably ask me to make him coffee

34

first.'

The night staff in Casualty were not encouraged to take their ease. There were no comfortable chairs. If there were quiet times they sat on the uniform, geometric little wooden chairs with scarcely any backs and not enough seat, or they desecrated the examination couches with their shining white sheets and pillowcases and folded blue blankets. Mark perched on a cold radiator, sipping his coffee, and asked, 'First job?'

'Yes,' Sheila told him. 'This is my internship year.'

'Of course, it must be. It seems years since mine.'

'Well, it *is* years. Five of them. You must have done a lot since then, but meeting you here, in St John's, is truly amazing.'

'Do you believe in fate, Sheila?'

'No, not really.'

'Nor I. It's pure coincidence. I mean if it *was* fate, our meeting up again, one would have to read something into it. It wouldn't just end here.'

Sheila tried to think she wasn't blushing. She looked at Mark as for the first time and had the same primary reactions. His lean face was so good-looking with its slightly aquiline nose and craggy chin, his eyes set as though in granite yet opening to a surprising softness that was the darkest of chestnut, his hair was almost black. His smile, when he smiled, was a little lopsided and endearing. She had always loved his smile.

He saw a girl he had loved and lost now matured into a very lovely young woman; her face was a bit thinner and her honey-coloured hair dressed more smoothly. She looked as though she had lost a little weight. Under her white coat her waist was tiny. She had also lost height, but this was due to the fact that she was wearing casual, flat-heeled comfortable shoes. She had used to tip-tap along beside him in the highest of heels.

'What happened to you?' Sheila urged him. 'I had no news of you whatever after you—er—left med. school.'

'Did you seek news of me?' he asked with genuine interest, but read in the lowering of her eyes and her sudden interest in her fingernails that this wasn't a fair question. She had simply wondered about him, asked the doctors who knew him if they had heard anything; a direct approach after the ending of a love affair was unthinkable.

'Well, where does one begin?' He had reverted to an impersonal tone. 'I started my internship at the Greater London Hospital, but I finished it at Kingsbury: I had by then decided to be a surgeon, so I attached myself to surgical firms. My father died when I was in my tenth month as an intern and my dreams of grandeur died with the fact that I was the family breadwinner. Dad didn't leave much and I was saddled with a mortgage.'

'I'm sorry about your father,' Sheila said quickly. 'I met him, if you remember, when he came for the presentation of diplomas ceremony.'

'So you did. He fancied you himself!' Mark's wry smile flashed out. 'Well, with the old boy gone I knew I had to take jobs in residence. Harley Street and general practice were out as I literally hadn't a bean in the world. I had the greatest incentive in the world to better my degree as I needed to earn more. I stayed on at Kingsbury as surgical houseman to Winthrop-Roberts, the abdominal surgeon, and studied like a demon for my MD.'

'Any girl-friends while at Kingsbury?' Sheila couldn't resist.

'Girl-friends? You must be joking! Somebody had just stamped all over my heart.' Her eyes glimmered a little, and he shrugged and proceeded, 'The odd one or two here and there, nothing serious. I decided, for some reason, to write my thesis on the spleen, and had a few sessions with the relevant consultants. I became really interested in my subject and felt that with it I was finding my true destiny. Fate—ah, that foolish word crops up again!—had a shock in store for me, however. Over a period of about a week I realised that I was living with what was becoming a misery of pain. I would wake up with a splitting headache and then my chest would cramp; I also had rheumaticky pains in my arms and shoulders. I worked and studied, feeling ever more rotten, until I collapsed at the feet of a passing physician who took me under his wing and pronounced that I had poliomyelitis.'

'Oh, no!' was torn from Sheila, and it didn't sound either casual or merely polite but as though it had happened to her.

'As I'd had all my jabs it was a fairly mild attack,' Mark went on, 'and it took me all of a month to realise this thing was actually happening to *me*. I suppose when one thinks of polio one imagines everything is desperation, both as regards pain and prognosis. But with me it was more of a bloody inconvenience. It hurt to breathe, but I was stuck with it because it was never at any point unbearable; it hurt when I raised my arms and my head mutely thundered all the while. That was it, and instead of writing my thesis I was stuck in an isolation unit unable to write, read or even to think for long. Mother was wonderful. At the age of fifty-two she simply went out and took a job and enjoyed it so much, she's still working. I was on bed rest for six months and then I started on a hellish programme called rehabilitation. I had lost grip in my hands and could see my career as a surgeon sailing off down every drain. Also I was a bad patient and baulked at some of the things they asked me to do, such as playing with plasticine.'

'Not playing,' Sheila corrected gently. 'It was manipulating your fingers.'

'I know that, but I wouldn't admit it. There was one woman who insisted I couldn't go home until I'd made a plasticine duck. It couldn't be a car or an engine, only a blooming duck. It had to be recognisable, with a flat bill and webbed feet. I told her I was a grown man, despite my physical shortcomings, and I wasn't making a duck for her or anybody. She said *she* was a grown woman, and would also admit to my manhood despite my childish behaviour, but these things had nothing to do with making a duck. It was my rehabilitation which required that I should make a duck. She had proved that there was quite a lot to a duck with its thin legs and broad, flat feet, not to mention the rounded head and wing feathers. She said I either wanted to become a surgeon or I didn't,

39

but arguing with physiotherapists only made me a bore. I'm inclined to stretch out the business about the plasticine duck because that was my first meeting with Jane—Jane Roberts—and I was prepared to make her a whole farmyard of ducks before I was much older.' He held out his hands and clenched and unclenched the fists. 'All this is thanks to Jane,' he said. 'She was more than my physiotherapist, she was an angel.'

Sheila had a sharp pain in her chest which she told herself was indigestion. Dinner had been particularly over-seasoned, the onions very strong.

'And did you—?'

Staff Nurse Collins poked her dark countenance round the door.

'Customers,' she announced. Sheila wanted to cry. She simply had to know about Mark and Jane before she could know another moment's peace of mind. Mark, however, was already striding after Nurse Collins to the reception hall where a woman was hugging a small child to her chest which was whining miserably and breathing in short gasps. A little distance away sat a well-dressed man blinking confusedly through a curtain of blood dripping down over his face from a series of jagged cuts in the bald dome of his head.

'You take that one,' Mark directed, 'and I'll see the child.'

The same young constable who had accompanied Mrs Esher stood by blushing a little as Sheila approached.

'Well, Constable, you're having a busy night shift. How did this happen?' She had nodded to Nurse Lewis, who was busy swabbing away the blood as she led the patient to a cubicle.

'I think he'd been celebrating, Doctor. He passed me once and said goodnight, obviously a bit inebriated but not offensive. Next thing I heard a crash and he'd walked through a plate-glass window—Garridges, in the High Street. He didn't seem too bad, so I brought him along here myself. I've been thinking I should have made him lie down, perhaps, and sent for the ambulance? This is my first night duty and—'

'Normally one should observe the rules, Constable, but the damage does appear to be mainly superficial. I think only one cut needs a couple of stitches. I hope you didn't leave Garridges wide open to looters?'

'No, Doctor. One of our cars was practically on the spot at the time.'

'I should go and get a cup of tea. When our friend is comfortable I'll tell you if he feels up to talking. I'll probably keep him here all

41

night in case of shock, so you needn't worry he'll run away.'

'Right, Doctor. I'll phone my sergeant where I am.'

When Mr Goodrich, stitched and plastered, was sipping hot weak tea and still wondering what had happened, Sheila phoned his wife to tell her not to worry, that her husband would be brought home in the morning. She had just replaced the instrument, not wishing to be drawn into a long harangue by a woman who was obviously dying to have a row with anybody in place of her celebrating spouse, when Mark called her.

'I need you,' he said crisply, and she knew he meant professionally. He looked grave and rather grim. 'Here we are in midsummer,' he scowled, 'and I have a kid with pleurisy which has developed into empyema. The mother tells me their flat is in a basement and the bedroom is covered in green mould most of the time. She's an unmarried mother, by the way, and takes the kid with her each day to a domestic service job she has. Her employer complained today about the youngster's crying and said she would have to leave if that sort of thing went on. When she finished her day's stint it was after surgery hours, so she decided to leave it till morning. Then the kid had a fit—the mother carried it to her doctor's

42

only to find he was out at a confinement, so she came on here. I don't know whether to have a fit myself or shriek blue murder against a society which can allow this sort of thing to happen, even in isolated circumstances.'

'What's to be done?' Sheila asked calmly.

'I phoned Sir William—he's my boss—and he said this is something I can well tackle myself. He doesn't see why he need come along. So if you'll watch the kid I'll call the RSO and warn the theatre staff. I—I've never operated on my own before and I'm a bit nervous.'

'You'll have the RSO standing by.'

'Yes. A pair of gimlet eyes watching everything I do wrong.'

'Or right,' Sheila smiled.

'Thanks. You've restored my sagging confidence.'

There was another quiet hour when Mark had gone off to the emergency theatre which was used at night, well away from the hospital proper so that comings and goings were neither disturbing nor disturbed by other hospital distractions. Night Sister Thanet paid a routine visit, scolded a student for having long hair, acidly enquired of the staff nurse if that was a *blood* stain on the floor, and if so, why; raked Sheila with a cold, mistrustful glance and went on her way.

'Frigid old hag,' was nurse's comment.

'Oh, now!' Sheila smiled. 'Sister has her job to do.'

'When they're that age, though, their job is simply looking for trouble,' said Collins. 'They say she used to be a beauty and in love with Dr Piper, but whatever went wrong he married somebody else. Now we all have to pay for her troubles—every night.'

'Oh, come, Staff Nurse, be fair. We didn't quite get rid of all Mr Goodrich's blood, now did we? And I think Sister is still very good-looking in a Mona Lisa way.'

'Of course you have to stick up for her. You're management, too, and we're only the workers. Which reminds me, where did Lewis get to? She can smell Sister coming a mile off and always leaves me to carry the can.'

Sheila smiled after the departing crisp white apron. A staff nurse was as jealous of her portion of 'management' in the hierarchy of the hospital as anybody else. She wondered how Mark was doing and what he had really felt about meeting her again. This was a time for seeing black as black and white as white; calling a spade a spade. It had all been new with Mark; the ecstasy of loving and the bottomless pit of despair.

'But I found Bruce and Mark met Jane,' Sheila told herself flatly. 'There isn't only one

44

person who's right for one. I would never have given Mark more than a passing thought if I hadn't bumped into him tonight.'

But having 'bumped', one suddenly remembered depths of feeling unsounded as the ocean. That had been the arguments, the quarrels, exuberant and whole-hearted. It was only when there was 'impasse' that despair had come into it: Mark who had to go and she who had to stay; there was no getting round that and they had been very wise to finish the business off quickly. The knife-thrust was always preferable to the drawn-out agony.

'Mark, come back soon,' Sheila breathed in a kind of desperation. 'Tell me all about you and Jane, that you married her and now have a couple of children. Then I can get on with my life in peace again.'

She walked round the department in case there were any casualties who had wandered in and been overlooked. Two of the students on standby duty were sitting in Outpatients, obviously bored. The other was reading up Neurology in the linen-closet.

'I should close your eyes,' Sheila advised them. 'It looks like being a long night and I'll call you if I need you.'

There were sounds of voices from the porter's cubbyhole and, glancing in, Sheila saw that the two ambulance attendants

45

together with Bill, the porter, and Tony, the Italian orderly, were playing cards. She looked again in some surprise.

'Where's Jock?' she enquired, looking at the only one of the quartet unknown to her.

'Oh, he went home while you were busy a while back, Doctor,' Phil explained. 'His wife phoned. The little girl hadn't come home from the pictures. He was no use to us worried like that, so I told him to go and I phoned the station for a replacement. This is Derek.'

'How d'you do,' Sheila nodded at the young ambulance attendant. 'Have you heard from Jock since?'

'No. I believe they were going to notify the police.'

'How worrying for them,' sighed Sheila. What did one do when one's child was late home? One waited, of course, watching the clock move through leaden seconds to make each minute, then one went out searching, trying not to panic. Round the next corner one would meet the child skipping happily and unharmed, completely unaware of the time or the desperation in a parent's heart. When one notified the police, that was an open declaration of that desperation. By that time one was really afraid . . .

*   *   *

46

Empty houses always fascinated little Mary Lindsay. She herself lived with her mummy and daddy and four brothers and sisters in a nice new Council flat not very far from the hospital and the ambulance station where Daddy worked, but she, the eldest, could still remember the little house where they used to live, one of many in a long row with cramped, cosy rooms, the wallpaper peeling off with damp, no bathroom, a large brown sink in the kitchen and an outside toilet which was known as the 'bogey-house', because the children took it in turns to scream 'bogey' at the one who was occupying the toilet at the time.

After the families had moved from Wells Street the houses were knocked down as though they were made of cards. Mary had watched their own old house demolished and cried because the flat had never become home as this had been. There was something obscene in seeing the yellow-papered front bedroom exposed to view, looking pathetically poky and squat, almost like a box, when Mummy had lain there and proudly displayed first Jimmy, then Tony, Annabel and Alex as dimpled babies to the critical eyes of the first-born herself.

It was much more fun seeing other people's

houses knocked down, and Mary, finding it still quite light on this summer night after the 'pictures', had gone to see what was happening to the big houses in River Grove; they had always been 'posh' houses and they did have bathrooms. Mary was not to know they stood in the path of a new bypass. To her it seemed such a waste. They were so much nicer than the Council flats.

Her friend had gone home, and Mary, knowing it was late, thought, 'I'll get murdered when I get home 'cause Dad's not there to stop her.' She was comfortably conscious of affinity with her father, would often play up to him and say something bright, knowing it would be repeated to his friends at the ambulance station.

There was one house with its front torn off and it looked almost as pathetic as Wells Street, only the paper was red and gold. Mary, with her slim little body, had broken through a gap in the fencing round the demolition site; when she thought about it she felt lonely, but she determined to take a closer peep at the ruin before going home.

'I'll bet it has banisters to slide down!' Mary thought, and climbed over a heap of rubble to stand inside the house itself. The interior was disappointing, for if there had been banisters they had been removed, as had most of the doors. There were sounds, too; creaking sounds and mouse patters and—and ghost whispers?

'I'm not afraid of ghosts!' Mary called clearly but waveringly. 'I'm going upstairs.' As the eldest of a family she had always to prove to herself that she was brave. She had quickly learned to sneer at the night-light Tony demanded, at Annabel's screams for comfort after a bad dream.

The stairs were creaky and inclined to sag even under her light weight. When she felt them giving way she didn't know they would bring with them the beam from the floor above, that these stolen moments of adventure would also steal the rest of her childhood away. She didn't know that when she became ten iron callipers would support her crushed limbs and that she—the eldest—would become the one who always watched what the others were doing. All she knew was that she hurt, and somehow the hurting made her go to sleep, and when she awoke it was dark and she hurt again.

★   ★   ★

'Mark!' Sheila exclaimed almost too gladly, her thoughts having become too grim to bear. 'How did it go, the op?'

'Oh, not too badly at all. I drew off nearly a pint of fluid and the kid stood up very well. I—I'm a nervous wreck at the moment, though.'

'Coffee?' she urged him. 'Just a moment, I'll ask Nurse. Then maybe we can continue our little chat.'

Before the coffee came, however, a small boy was dragged in, whimpering, holding a dirty, swollen forefinger up for inspection.

'Don't cut it! Don't!' he yelped.

'A whitlow, I think, Mr Leighton?' she winked at Mark. 'I think I'd better attend to it while you get your breath back. OK?'

'Don't cut my finger! *Don't!*' shouted the boy.

'Shut up or I'll clip you one,' his loving mother adjured him.

'I think sonny and I will have a short session together in here with Nurse,' said Sheila, indicating the septic-room.

'But you're not going to cut it, are you?'

'I promise not to do anything you don't want me to.'

Nurse Collins drew up the trolley containing the sterilised instruments.

'Well, young man, and what have you done to yourself?'

'He's got a fine whitlow, Nurse, and we're just going to wash his hands for a start. Can you do that—and watch that finger? It feels like a house-side at the moment, doesn't it, sonny?'

'You're not going to cut it, are you, Doc? Don't cut it!'

'Well,' Sheila conceded, 'if I can't cut it will you let me have just a small prick? Fair's fair, and I've got to do something. I'm a doctor.'

'Er—will a prick make it stop 'urting?'

'That I can promise you,' she assured the child.

She felt him jerk as the cocaine needle pierced deeply and then released the numbing drug. After a minute he said happily, 'It's stopped 'urting. Can't feel a ruddy thing.'

'Right.' This was the moment one had sweetly to deceive, however. She took the arm under her own and held it over a bowl, so that the child couldn't see what was happening for her body. She winked at Nurse Collins, who began to chatter about Jamaica. The lancet pierced, bringing no response from the sufferer. At that moment the throbbing finger was a dead digit as far as feeling was concerned. A thick ooze of blood and pus poured into the waiting bowl and as Sheila squeezed slightly the boy saw what had happened.

'You cut it!' he accused, his eyes round.

'I know. I didn't promise not to. I said I'd

51

only do what you wanted and I knew you'd want me to in the end. Anyway, you didn't feel anything, and it's going to be fine now. You can tell all the other boys tomorrow that you've had an operation.'

'Hey, you're not a bad doc for a woman. I didn't feel a thing—honestly.'

'Well, thanks for the compliment, but don't send all your pals to me. Nurse will put a bandage on that lot and make it look important. OK?'

Fresh coffee was served as the phone rang in the department. The students rallied and gathered. They rather hoped they were going out to the scene of an accident to relieve the boredom of the night.

'Right!' Mark spoke into the receiver. 'We'll come at once. We'll bring our own ambulance.'

Sheila was waiting, her eyes questioning.

'They've found Jock's wee girl,' he said quietly. 'Down near the river in a derelict house. A beam has fallen on her. She may be damaged, but not—thank God!—in the way I think we both imagined.'

'It's funny,' Sheila said in relief as they bowled along, 'how one is inclined to think the worst.'

Still, it was a bad enough business. Mary was such a little girl and the beam pinning her down was so big. When they eventually extricated her and saw her contused and distorted limbs it seemed doubtful she would ever walk, let alone run and play again. The healers of the night took it all in their stride as a job to be done along with other jobs. They also had to take Jock in hand, too, and sedate him. The mother remained wonderfully calm. Women, at times when courage is needed, have a habit of surprising even themselves.

★　　　★　　　★

Sheila trailed off duty as the ebullient Dr Merritt relieved her, not knowing whether she was on her head or her heels and not too sure she liked night duty.

Now the hospital was all agog and athrong with people—it had appeared that Casualty was the only place awake at night—and was the drama always so acute as she had experienced for her initiation? At least there had been no fatalities, which was something, but the business about little Mary Lindsay had been horrid. Hurt and terrified, the child had closed her mind to outward events, had even looked upon her own mother and father as strangers. Still, she would live, and maybe life would heal her emotional disturbances in time. But what about Mrs Esher? If she was determined she would finish the job she had started next time, if there was a next time.

Now that she could go to bed if she wished, Sheila felt suddenly wide awake and curious about the patients she had handled in the night. She would ask after them and then go to her room, her mind at rest on certain scores.

Mrs Esher was in a side-ward attached to Women's Surgical; blood was still feeding into her veins and she looked as though she was sleeping naturally. Her husband, Gerald, sat close by, his eyes heavy from lack of sleep and unnaturally bright.

'I should go home and get some rest, Mr Esher,' Sheila advised. 'I'm sure they'll let you know as soon as there's any change in your wife's condition.'

'I couldn't rest away from her, Doctor, so I would rather stay. I've been told I may.'

'Oh, very well. But we can't have you falling ill . . .'

'I didn't know I could cry, Doctor. Can you believe that? But seeing my wife like this has been a revelation to me. It's as though I've rediscovered emotion. I know I'm upset and talking far too much, but I don't care. I have a great desire to relieve my mind by saying a good deal.'

'I should remember that when your wife

wakes up. Say things to her you've been keeping secret. Most people are far too reticent about their emotional relationships.'

In the children's surgical ward Sheila once more bumped into Mark. He had gone off duty half an hour ahead of her to see his post-operative patient.

'How is Carol?' she asked.

'Holding her own at the moment. With a long history of pneumonia, however, her prognosis isn't all that good. I shan't go to bed until Sir William has seen her.'

'Have you had breakfast yet?'

'No.'

'Neither have I.'

She waited, hoping he would suggest they breakfast together, but he stood gazing down at wee Carol's cot and the day staff were obviously on edge with two doctors blocking the ward.

'Well, I'll see you tonight if not before,' Sheila said as she turned away.

'Yes. Sleep well,' he advised her, and gave his lopsided smile. 'We never did finish our chat, did we?'

'Lots of time,' she assured him, and went off feeling strangely bereft at leaving him behind, as though her life would exist in a hiatus until she saw him again.

She breakfasted alone, though five other

young medicos shared the large table. One had only to open a book and pretend to be reading it to be left out of the conversation. It must have been tiredness, but she was beset by a weight of problems suddenly. Going on duty last evening she hadn't been aware of any, and her mother had lately been much more friendly and understanding. Her problems—she faced them squarely—had arisen from meeting up with Mark again. She hadn't, after all, forgotten him or his effect upon her. She didn't want things to be as they had been, of course, because she had matured and fallen in love with Bruce, as Mark had learned to love Jane. The trouble was that there had been no progression in her affair with Mark. When things had begun to seem impossible they had finished, whereas had they gone on there would probably have been a slow deterioration in the relationship and a conclusion drawn clearly in black and white. When one's memories are mostly wonderful one is inclined to label the experience so; but it wouldn't be as wonderful as that a second time. It couldn't be. Sad as was this conclusion, it was, unfortunately, the truth.

★   ★   ★

Elaine Esher opened her eyes, saw Gerald

eyeing her in a peculiar, imploring way, traced the tube from her arm to the vacolitre of blood on the stand above and remembered.

'Gerald, I didn't mean it. I'm sorry. I didn't mean it.'

'That's all right, Elaine. I should have come home. It was my fault.'

'No, Gerald,' she didn't know how her bandaged hand had crept into his. They hadn't held hands for years. Even their now-neglected intimate moments had been performed without unnecessary familiarities. 'You must feel free to stay out if you have to. I was silly and it was wrong. I did it to frighten you, only you weren't there.'

'I was frightened, Elaine. I still am.' He began to blubber like a baby.

'Why, Gerald? You don't really care—about me?'

'Don't say that. I thought you'd gone a bit off, old thing, but it was awful thinking you might never be there. It's nice thinking you're at home even when I'm at the club.'

'You never told me that.'

'No. I'm telling you now and I hope you'll remember. There's only you, and—and that's enough.'

'I know I haven't been well, Gerald, and I should have gone to a doctor. You were right. I—I lost my perspective all at once. I suppose they'll treat me like a loonie now?'

'I shouldn't think so.' He squeezed her hand encouragingly. 'We've probably both just come to our senses. Did you know you have an unusual blood-grouping?'

'No. I never thought about it. I suppose that added to the general inconvenience?'

'I'll say! There was a nice little doctor who looked after you. She had the same grouping and she was prepared to offer her services, but they managed to get what they needed from another hospital. Anyway, how are you feeling now, dear?'

'In a funny, guilty way I'm feeling happy, Gerald. I suppose that's wicked of me?'

'Not at all. I feel much, much happier now. I didn't want to understand what was happening until last night you brought us both down to bedrock. Now I know I just want to live with you through all your phases. Mention another woman to me again and I'll probably blow up.'

Elaine lay back contentedly and Sister, seeing the change in her patient, indicated to Gerald that he could safely leave his wife in the hospital's hands.

CHAPTER FOUR

Sheila Devaney slept like a log for five hours and then she knew she had had it. For a while she lay listening to all the sounds of the day near at hand; the whine of lifts and the clatter of dustbin lids and trolleys; further away the traffic made a steady hum which became a roar as one concentrated on it; jets roared through the sky towards the airport and the June sunlight was piercingly bright even through the drawn chintz curtains with their pattern of ivy-leaves and darting lovebirds.

She slid out of bed and drew back the curtains. Gardeners were busy hoeing the rose-beds and beyond two lively games were taking place on the tennis-courts. She watched these for a moment wondering if she was up to a game herself. Behind came a stealthy, apologetic tap on the door.

'Yes?' Sheila poked her face round to see Tilly, the corridor maid, regarding her.

'I hope I didn't wake you, Doctor?'

'No, Tilly, I was awake. What is it?'

'Well, Mr Leighton told me to see if you were stirring. He's having a cup of tea in the canteen and wondered if you would care to join him.'

'I'll be along in ten minutes, Tilly.'

Funny how eagerly she showered and dressed in one of her favourite dresses, blue cotton with pleats and a sailor collar with broad white bands. Mark was lounging against the canteen counter and his dark eyes glowed to see her.

'I didn't literally mean join me here in the canteen,' he smiled. 'I thought we might go out and find a cottage garden with strawberry teas?'

'Sounds lovely,' she told him. 'You know, I'd forgotten it's the strawberry season out there. If you hadn't mentioned it I might have been deprived for a whole year. Couldn't you sleep, either?'

'No. It takes time to settle down from one's diurnal practices. It's not enough that one comes off duty feeling dead beat. One's mind is locked in habit. Are you ready?'

'Yes. How are we going?'

'I've borrowed Martha Haley's MG. Know her?'

'Yes, vaguely. She's a very glamorous brunette.'

'And my immediate boss; Sir William's registrar. As you'll have gathered, at the moment I haven't a car.'

She was about to say, 'We can take mine,' but desisted. Men are proud creatures and do not accept favours with grace.

They went vaguely countrywards out of the meandering city, without discussing a particular route. When it becomes less important to know where one is going than with whom one is travelling, then one is in dangerous or delightful company and it is as well to watch out.

'Thorley Woods,' announced Mark eventually after they had remarked on the progress of hay-making and the preponderance of wild roses on the hedgerows. 'I believe we can park the car here and take a footpath through the woods and that one eventually comes to a smallholding where the good wife makes teas. Of course she may be out marketing or visiting friends. Risk it?'

'Of course. A walk through the woods is worth the effort.'

'And you can tell me what happened to you since we last met,' he prompted.

'Not until you've finished your story. You were being manipulated back to usefulness by a persistent young lady named Jane who was really an angel. Remember?'

'Yes,' that endearing lopsided smile, 'I remember. Doesn't leaf-mould smell like a million? And it must be the answer to humanity's suffering feet. "Have your house carpeted in leaf-mould and save your bunions!" Whoops, I nearly lost my attentive listener there.' He reached out a sinewy arm and hauled her out of a bramble patch. The touch of his hand sent little needles of awareness screaming mutely through her body and made her self-conscious.

'I can manage, thanks,' she said rather shortly, pretending to be annoyed about her laddered tights. 'I must learn to look where I'm going.'

'Jane,' he began indulgently, as one speaks of the past, 'was so good for me it simply wasn't true. She was feminine and yet she was strong, she manipulated me as though I was a puppet and she seemed to sense I was ripe for a love affair and that she fitted the role of sweetheart to perfection. I say "role" because I believe that is what it was to Jane. She was always playing a part, the theme of which was "Mark must pick up his career exactly where he left off". She played it to perfection, I must say, and it was a most enjoyable six months. Then I had to sever my dependence on her; in other words our relationship had to mature with me in the dominant role bossing Jane around a little as her future lord and master. This play wasn't much of a success and we had to take it off after a couple of months, I regret to say. Jane just wasn't the type one could boss. She bossed back and there were a number of head-on collisions, the cause of one of these being a certain gentleman who had crashed his racing car and needed the Jane treatment to give him confidence to join the circuit again. I could see myself in that laddie, being bullied by a female who knew darned well how to get her way with her patients. I don't say Jane was his sweetheart, too, but she was just as sweet to him in a pleading, cajoling, "do it just for me" sort of way until he was safely launched into the world again. I decided it was time to throw down the gauntlet with my lady. "Jane," I said, "I think we should get married as soon as possible. What do you say?" "Rubbish!" she said quite firmly. "We'd fight like a cat and dog and you know it. I don't think I'm the marrying kind, Mark. I'm involved with too many people. I simply can't canalise myself. I would like to be a wife, naturally, but I should hate being married," which was a typical sort of Jane reasoning, if you can follow it. I regret to say I shed not one single tear. Either one becomes hard or one doesn't cry a second time.'

Sheila caught his eye and there was a lump in her throat. Had he cried—in his man's way—as much as she had the first time?

'And then?' she prompted quickly.

'I think yonder lies our cottage. Let's see if we're going to be lucky before I continue with this epic on non-events which has been my life to date.'

They were indeed lucky. The smallholder's wife was delighted to see Mark again.

'With a different young leddy!' was her teasing, tantalizing remark, which made Sheila's brows shoot up.

'Jane?' she asked naughtily.

'No.' He gave a laughing shrug. 'Can I help being popular?'

There was home-made brown bread and white bread, thick with butter; wheaten scones and sultana buns and a spiced loaf with whole walnuts spilling out; gooseberry jam and rhubarb and ginger preserve and a vast mound of freshly-picked strawberries with a pint jug of whipped cream. Lastly there was a large brown teapot, big enough for a family, sending out a curl of blue steam.

'Is there to be an execution?' Sheila asked reverently.

'This is the way sensible people always live,' Mark said blandly. 'It's living in hospital which makes one imagine that all food is *ersatz*. Eat and enjoy, but don't broadcast this to your friends. Mrs Billings only obliges me.'

'And of course, your favoured companion of the moment,' Sheila couldn't resist.

'If that's so very important, she was staff nurse on St Vincent's Ward, a big red-headed girl, and I was best man at her wedding in January to an ENT man.'

'Oh. I didn't mean to pry it out of you. Sorry!'

'You did, and you're not at all sorry. I, too, am interested in every chap who's kissed you, though I may add it's against my will.'

She took time to work this out and then she said, 'Go on about your career—your story.'

'Oh, it was hard work and graft. I'd lost two and a half years and I had a lot of catching up to do. I eventually was taken on Sir William Bender's firm as senior house-surgeon and I'm preparing a thesis for my MD. I have really slogged and this work is now almost ready for the typist. I'm beginning to feel in my bones an itch to relax, which is why I'm here with you today.'

'What are your prospects if you get your MD? Should I say *when* you get it?'

'That's right, have a bit of faith in me. Sir William wants me to stay with him and change hospitals. He has a couple of consultancies and a private clinic. He's a man who knows his subject and can help one quite a lot. He's also getting on, so I presume he'll retire eventually and then prospects will be truly rosy.'

'You might even be able to get a car of your own.'

'I'm thinking of buying this MG, actually. Martha's tired of it and is offering it in part exchange for a Porsche she's got her eye on.'

'Who's Martha?'

'The glamorous brunette, I think you said? My boss, in other words.'

'And Martha in your own. You call your boss Martha?'

'What's that supposed to involve? I call her Martha when we're out socially, by request. Being my boss she calls me Mark at all times.'

'Do you see her a lot, socially?' Sheila knew such questions and answers could only hurt and yet she pursued them, determined to flagellate herself.

'No. As I told you I've been working rather hard recently. Anyhow, my story is now up to date. Or almost up to date,' he added more seriously. 'Very recently I met up again with my old sweetheart—or would it be more gallant to say my sweetheart of olden time? Did Mark and Sheila live happily ever after?' he demanded of the room in general. 'Had love stood the test of time? Don't forget to read the next instalment of our gripping romantic serial!'

'I don't think you need joke about it,' Sheila said in injured tones.

'I'm not joking. Now it's I who am fishing. Why do you think I'm here at this moment sharing this wonderful spread with you?'

'Because you enjoy wonderful spreads?' Sheila ventured.

'Oh, I do. But I could have enjoyed this particular spread alone. I asked you along because I wanted to be with you.'

'Thanks!'

'Now you're supposed to say you like being with me, but only if it's true.'

'I think it's true.'

'Ha, ha! She refuses to commit herself.'

'You know it's true. You also know I'm rather shy. I can't say things like that very often.'

'You're blushing. You always did.'

'Five years is a long time.'

'You're trying to tell me it's you that got married?'

'Good lord! I've been grinding away all this time. I only started my internship in March.'

'We seem to have depleted the food stocks to Mrs Billings' satisfaction. Do you think we could go now?'

'If you're ready.'

Every word, every gesture was heavy with implication. Sheila knew she should have said, 'I'm engaged to be married,' but she didn't, and yet she knew she was rapidly approaching a furnace door which could burn them both up to cinders if they followed these inviting, investigatory paths to their conclusion.

The woodland was soft and quiet in the distilled golden light of early evening and there was a breathlessness about it. It happened as Sheila tripped down a rabbit hole. In the middle of her laughter her lips were silenced and she knew they were where they belonged, pressed hard against Mark's. The realisation was paralysing coupled with the sheer physical capitulation of the kiss itself. Precious minutes which were a whole eternity passed and then Mark spoke shakily.

'It seems there is fate, Sheila, at this moment, busily knitting together the pattern we mutually abandoned.'

She sighed deeply as though coming out of an anaesthetic.

'We have to go,' he said in some dismay. 'How about just one more for the road?'

She pulled away from him sharply. 'Mark, I can't. I don't want to.'

He tried to search her countenance for teasing. She looked extremely serious, however.

'Darling, don't blow hot and cold with me after all this time! We've both done a lot of growing up. I think we just proved that. We can't play kiss and run away any longer.'

'I'm not running away, but I'm not kissing, either.'

'Oh.' He had his pride, and women were notoriously fickle jades. 'Well, whatever else we decide to do we have to get back to the hospital and work. This time watch where you're putting your feet.'

She felt dreadful. All the enchantment was gone and there was Mark's familiar figure grown haughty and faintly hostile. He must be thinking she had led him on simply to reject him once again. She hated women who played with their power over men for the hell of it. Why couldn't she have told him when he had asked if she was married, 'No, but I am engaged'? Then he would have known where he stood and kept the whole tone of their present relationship quite friendly but impersonal. She had deliberately suppressed news of Bruce because she had wanted to be in Mark's arms once more; she had secretly known the whole afternoon's capers were leading to that inevitable end unless she herself cried out 'halt!' in good time.

Now that she had said it, it had created a chasm between them and small talk was not sufficient to bridge it. Maybe it would be easier to mention Bruce when they had both forgotten that recent breathless merging a little; maybe two doctors in their white duty coats, in the sterile atmosphere of Casualty, would be in a mood better to assimilate cold facts and put emotional outbursts and expressions in their proper place.

She heard herself going on about the car as they drove back to the city, as though it mattered.

'It would be nice for you to have this car. You handle it very well. I wonder why this Martha person wants to sell it?'

'She likes variety. She's a woman.'

There was a sting in that somewhere, but Sheila pressed on.

'It must be grand to be registrar to somebody like Sir William, and beautiful into the bargain. I think I heard he was a bachelor?'

'He's not thinking of marrying Martha,' came quite shortly. 'He didn't select her for her sex or her beauty. She happens to be clever and extremely efficient.'

'I didn't mean ...' Sheila muttered miserably, and gave the subject up. How could one indulge in gossip after a desperation of stolen happiness which had now turned to misunderstanding and misery? They were approaching the hospital before she spoke again.

'I wonder who, at this moment, is planning, consciously or unconsciously, to keep us busy tonight?'

'Yes, I wonder.' He had relaxed minimally.

'Thanks for a lovely afternoon, Mark. It was unexpected and I did enjoy it.'

'Yes, it was very good in parts. Thanks for your company.'

He parked the car and hastened to let her out of the passenger door. 'See you later,' he said with a small, mocking salute, and was gone.

She felt both miserable and guilty as she changed her laddered tights and prepared for supper and another spell of duty. Bruce was heavy on her conscience. How could one go ahead and marry the man to whom one was engaged when one has just proved that one was still in love with somebody else? Bruce had done nothing wrong, neither had he changed. He was sweet and considerate and she now knew where he fitted in her life. He was the living replacement of the father she had adored. She knew she could make Bruce happy: after enjoying his bachelor life he was suddenly feeling the itch to have a child of his own; they had planned quite frankly not to delay this enterprise longer than necessary. But where did her plain duty now lie? Should she go ahead with Bruce without mentioning her heart's alarming defection? Should she mention it and put the ball into his court, asking if he wished to keep her to their contract in spite of it? Or should she tell Bruce that she simply couldn't go on and marry him, even though there was no future for her with Mark, either?

'I wish I'd never met up with Mark again!' she cried out in desperation. 'Everything was all settled and the prospect comfortable and pleasing. Now I feel as though I've been in the path of a tornado and nothing whole is left in my life.'

She was tired even as she sought a place in the dining-room and there were dark shadows beneath her eyes. Only last evening she had written to Bruce telling him about her prospective night duty. He would have received that letter and maybe replied to it, or maybe not. He was on holiday and fishing; he wouldn't think there was any haste or anticipate any crisis in his life. She couldn't spoil his holiday in any case. When he came back there would have to be a confessional— she was too honest not to tell him what had happened and admit her own weakness in the matter.

CHAPTER FIVE

'Who is Sheila?' asked Martha Haley, bending familiarly over Mark's chair, her eyes like twin emeralds. There was an admiring silence from Mark Leighton's table companions; it wasn't every day a beautiful registrar breathed so agreeably upon one of their number. Registrars were labelled senior residents and had their dining-room elsewhere.

'Sheila?' Mark echoed, looking like an imbecile temporarily while he tried to decide what had prompted Martha's curiosity.

'Yes, Sheila. S.H.E.I.L.A.'

'Oh. She's a girl I used to know in my med school days. She's here now. Just fancy'—he included his table companions in the conversation—'she's been here since March and we've only just seen each other. Quite a fantastic size, this place. I sometimes think I'll meet everybody I ever knew if I stay long enough.'

The young men had all been standing politely since Miss Haley had joined them. She now handed over a lace-edged handkerchief to Mark.

'I found this in my car. It's too pretty to lose. Are you likely to see the lady again or shall I leave it in Lost Property?'

'Oh, we're in Cas together. I'll return it.'

Mark felt strangely rattled as Martha left that she should have made a public enquiry out of the returning of a mere handkerchief. Anybody else would quietly have disposed of the thing, pretty or not. He felt strongly that Martha minded his having another woman passenger in her car, and she had no right to. She had lent it unreservedly with a view to his trying it out, and what he did or whom he was with had nothing whatever to do with the proposed transaction they planned together. He was beginning to get the idea that Martha regarded him as a piece of her property; she swooped on him whenever they were in the same vicinity like a mother bird claiming her own, and during rounds she included him in the coterie surrounding Sir William, while pointedly snubbing the other house-surgeons and keeping them in their places. He became more resentful as he pondered, though no doubt the turn of the day's events had helped his mood to sour more quickly than usual, and wondered why the hell it should matter to Martha Haley who Sheila was or had been or even would be. At that moment he was definitely a woman-hater.

Sheila was miserably aware of Mark's presence in the large dining-room on this evening. She could even see him, for once, laughing a great deal with the group at his table. It suddenly struck her that there must have been many occasions when they had been in that room together, unknowing and so unsearching of the sea of faces present for the familiar countenance of dear, past love. It was, indeed, a capricious fate which had thrown them together in the course of their common work, and but for that they might have passed on, unaware, like ships in the night, getting on with their lives and new loves.

Jealousy stabbed Sheila's heart with a dagger-thrust as she saw the glamorous Martha Haley pause at Mark's table and engage him in conversation. What a wonderful couple they made, and how other people must be thinking the same thing! The two dark heads, one only a little above the other, for Martha was tall for a woman, and the rather obvious intimacy of the woman's long, slim surgeon's hand resting on Mark's tweed sleeve.

Hadn't Mark rushed in, rather, to deny any sexual interest between Sir William and his registrar? Did that mean he had ever thought there might be something between himself and Martha? Miss Haley looked the type who would further her husband's career to the best of her considerable ability; perhaps it was she who had persuaded Sir William to take Mark under his professional wing. Perhaps it had proved as great an inconvenience for Mark to meet up with Sheila as it had been for her; perhaps he, too, was wishing her a thousand miles away at this moment.

★   ★   ★

Luke Coventry believed in keeping fit. What had started as a rather good idea at forty had become a bit of an obsession at forty-eight. He liked to think he could still do all he had been able to do at twenty-five, which meant walking a mile in just over twelve minutes, playing a brisk game of squash after office hours before catching the train home, walking his mile instead of using the car and then settling down to a meal and a pretence at gardening before retiring to the local for a couple of pints well-earned and deserved before bed.

Beth, Luke's wife, was rather bored by Luke's efforts at keeping fit. She had borne him three sons, all now married, and her figure sagged and spread in all directions. He would sometimes say, teasingly, 'Old girl, you're dying of poisoning, you know.' She had risen the first time and asked, alarmed,

'Whatever do you mean?' 'I was reading an article this morning,' he explained, 'and it said if you compared every surplus pound of weight with a dose of arsenic you wouldn't be far out. You, my girl, are pretty far gone at that rate.' He had patted his own flat stomach with profound self-satisfaction. 'You make light of my keeping fit,' he proceeded, 'but I'll bet *you* can't wear clothes you had ten years ago.' Beth had acidly replied that ten years ago she was still wearing the clothes she had had ten years before that. 'You weren't exactly a millionaire when I married you and now that we're a bit better off I enjoy my food. You aren't going to talk me out of that, and I'm not exactly two-ton Tessie.' She wasn't. She had rounded everywhere, including her face. She looked middle-aged and didn't mind, whereas Luke liked to think he was in the very prime of his life and proved it almost every minute of the day, watching his waistline and making his muscles earn their keep.

On this day there was a board meeting which Luke was expected to attend as his firm's accountant. He hated board meetings because they went on for hours and hours; the directors didn't even have a proper lunch-break but had coffee and sandwiches sent in. Luke had a sharp attack of indigestion half an hour after eating the sandwiches and was miserable for the rest of the meeting, tasting the strong black coffee again and again as his stomach threw it back into his mouth. Last evening after a particularly strenuous game of squash with young Hopfield, the Northern representative, he had had a similar attack. It wasn't often his stomach gave him trouble and he hadn't felt quite as fit ever since. He hadn't told Beth, of course, because she didn't bother about keeping fit and had a digestion like a goat. She would probably have laughed. He felt vaguely miserable for the rest of the afternoon and blamed the sedentary nature of the past hours for this. Normally he would have spent his lunch hour walking twice round the square, called at the tavern for a bowl of soup and a roll and carried on happily until his evening's burst of activity. For once he would have liked to have cut squash, but this was all the more reason for being strong-minded and forcing himself.

Before the meeting broke up Ferguson, the Sales Director, said, 'Oh, Luke, come round to my place about six to wet my grandson's head. First one, you know. As proud as though it was our own.' Luke was a grandfather twice over, though he hadn't thought to wet those tiny heads convivially with his fellow directors.

Though Luke would have liked his evening

to run to its usual pattern; squash at the club, train, walk from the station, a relaxing drink, supper with Beth and then a stroll round the garden with the secateurs in his hand at the ready to rip off a weak shoot or an overblown rose, a final walk to the Prince Edward and then home to bed; he couldn't refuse old Ferguson. He phoned Beth that he would be an hour late, and explained, then went resolutely to the club where for half an hour he leapt about like a dervish and had to stop with a bad attack of stitch in his right arm. After a shower he felt more or less recovered and walked a mile to Ferguson's flat, finding London pavements a darned sight harder than those at home. There was everything to drink at the head-wetting but beer, and Luke hated spirits, not having a head for strong drink. He felt muzzy as he walked to the Underground and vomited in the Gents there. 'I can't be developing an ulcer,' he told himself uncomfortably as he changed stations and discovered he had just missed the Garstone train. There wasn't another for an hour. He phoned Beth once more and she said, 'Well, I'm not waiting any longer. I'm hungry. Shall I meet your train at nine with the car?' Luke, tempted, cast temptation aside. 'No. The exercise will do me good,' he asserted, 'and give me an appetite.'

As he turned away to read the evening paper he again had a stitch. For a moment it passed from his arm round his chest and back again. He felt the hair rise on his scalp and the skin on his face drew tightly across the bones. He suddenly wanted desperately to get home and tell Beth, but a few moments later the idea of his being ill seemed absurd.

Jogging along in the train Luke badly wanted a drink of water. He had never been as thirsty for water in all his life before, but there was no hope of getting any until he was home. The trains were slower at this time of evening and made many more stops than during the rush-hour. He willed the stations to arrive and pass and almost tumbled out of the train at Garstone. It had never looked so good to him before. He walked briskly, his thirst having subsided, sniffing the garden smells and drinking in the clean air greedily.

'Evening!' someone greeted.

Luke responded and turned into Bona Vista Avenue. The houses were some distance apart and 'Oakhaven' was at the far end. He had been slower than his usual twelve minutes; must be slipping. His steps speeded up to meet the challenge and then the stitch came again, only this time it was fierce and squeezed the air out of his chest in a terrifying embrace. Luke paused and dragged breath into his lungs agonisingly. He went on again, more slowly, half anticipating more hurt. It came as he reached his own gateway and staggered within for privacy to suffer what was happening to him. Beth, wearing her gardening gear and with her hair escaping from its bun, saw the livid countenance and cried out:

'My God, Luke, what's the matter?'

He found he couldn't speak. The world of house, garden and wife dissolved in a cascade of unbelievable pain as he slid to his knees and fell with his head against the green of freshly cut lawn-grass.

*   *   *

Sheila had just demonstrated to a lively young student how one excised a painful boil. The youth so afflicted had several old hard little cores already on his sallow neck. Sometimes it is painful to be young in every conceivable way.

'Put a clean, dry dressing on that,' Sheila advised the student as the worst of the ooze was wiped away. 'Watch you don't stick the plaster on growing hair.'

Since the night staff had taken over there had been a crop of minor casualties to deal with, including a boy bitten by a dog, a man with a cinder in his eye, a mother towing her young daughter who was suffering from a nose-bleed and a girl who had been stung by a bee and whose groin was beginning to swell ominously. Then the youth with the boil who insisted that he hadn't been able to attend his doctor's surgery because of a more pressing engagement! When pressed to say what this had been he became shy, however, so one presumed a lady had been involved, but with pleasure spent pain was a gloomier outlook, so he had sought relief at the hospital.

Mark was dealing with the bee-sting case in another room. He had greeted her most cheerfully, as though he hadn't seen her for twenty-four hours, and there hadn't been a chance of a private chat for which she felt only half relieved. Matters could not be allowed to remain in mid-air between them. Whatever Mark was thinking of her and her sudden *volte-face*, he had at least the right to be acquainted with the truth.

They finished with their patients together and Nurse Collins said somewhat aggressively: 'Are you ready for coffee yet, Doctors? I must warn you I'm on my own tonight. Lewis is having her night off and the relief is down with gastro-enteritis and so far they haven't sent me a replacement. Also Sister Thanet is excused duty owing to illness in the family—her mother, I believe. If there's a new broom on duty she'll be sure to sweep clean and it'll take me all my time to keep the department tidy. So—'

'Thank you, Nurse, we can make our own coffee when we want it,' Sheila cut her short. 'Do whatever you should be doing and use the students. That's what they're here for.' She turned to Mark. 'Would you like some refreshments?'

'Why not?' he returned. 'Are you domesticated?'

'I wouldn't know, but I can make coffee and boil eggs. You wouldn't care for a boiled egg, would you?'

'No, thanks. A couple of benzedrine tablets might come in handy, though.'

He followed her into the small kitchen next to Casualty Sister's locked office. There was no percolator or such refinements. The coffee was the instant variety and one simply boiled a kettle and added milk and sugar if required.

'By the way, I think apologies are in order,' he said suddenly. 'No offence intended and none taken, I hope?'

'What are you apologising for?' she asked blankly.

'You haven't forgotten my bull-like trespass on the grass this afternoon? I have this conceited notion that my attentions are invariably welcome and I appreciate your shooting me down.'

'I didn't intend to shoot you down,' she said in a low, embarrassed voice, 'and there's no need to apologise for your part in our encounter. I knew perfectly well what was going to happen and I invited it.'

'You mean I'm not anathema, then?' He looked considerably relieved and cheered. 'I was beginning to think I needed a certain soap as we renewed our acquaintance, and then you cried enough so suddenly. I've been quite upset, you know.' He groped for her hand and squeezed. 'Now say it was all right and send me out to my next job a happy man.'

She unscrewed her hand self-consciously. It burned from touching him. She held it out. It had been squeezed white, but on the third finger gleamed a triple diamond ring set in platinum and white gold.

'That's the reason I couldn't go on,' she explained in a shaky voice. 'I'm engaged to be married. It happened at Christmas. It's I who should apologise for letting things go so far.'

He bit his lip and turned away. She was desperately sorry for him, his manly pride shattered twice in one day. 'You knew you— and yet you—' His face twisted into a sardonic smile. 'You took me for a lovely ride, Doctor,' he told her. 'Tell me, is it true that stolen kisses are sweeter?'

'Oh, Mark, don't be bitter. I was wrong and I admit it. I wanted to enjoy our afternoon together. It was—was like old times.'

'A bit too much for comfort, if you ask me. I happened to think you were prepared to— carry on. I rather put my heart and soul into the effort.'

'I'm sorry,' she repeated rather sharply. She couldn't be disloyal to Bruce and say that her heart and soul had unaccountably become involved also in that emotional interlude.

'Well, sadder and wiser, I suppose,' he shrugged. 'By the way, you dropped this in the car.' He returned the handkerchief Martha had found from his breast pocket. 'You really shouldn't do things like that,' he added ambiguously, and walked out of the kitchen without his coffee.

It was no time to pester him with offers of refreshment. She had just handed him a very bitter brew indeed.

It spoke well for professional discipline that these two, unhappy and emotionally shattered, should feel a mutual, immediate concern for the figure which now entered their department on a stretcher trolley. Luke Coventry had recovered somewhat, and was inclined to be apologetic for his presence there and mode of transport.

'Damme!' he said. 'I had a couple and I suppose I was stewed for a moment and fell down. It does happen, you know, and I wasn't driving or anything like that. The wife here panics and I'm poked and probed by a doctor and then sent here like a bloomin' invalid on one of these things. I feel absoballylootly ridiculous. I'm renowned for my fitness. Anybody will tell you.'

'Dr Wade sent this letter,' Beth Coventry said tersely, 'and take no notice of him. When he staggered home he wasn't drunk, he was dying.'

'Ha, ha!' he chortled. 'That's what they call living in hopes, my dear. You know I've left the mortgage and all that to you in my will. You're on a loser either way.'

'Would you please lie still and not talk, Mr Coventry?' Mark asked as the ambulance men transferred the stretcher to an examination couch.

'My dear fellow—'

'No, seriously, Mr Coventry, keep still and be quiet.' Mark had a way of getting across to most people and Luke subsided, still thinking it all rather unnecessary but prepared to enjoy the novelty of being thought an invalid.

'Dr Wade wants a full electrocardiograph,' Mark told his colleague. 'While I'm listening in would you see if Dr Cafferty is available with his machine? If not, the operator will tell you who's available to do an ECG at this time of night.'

Sheila went off to telephone. Work, at times, was a godsend.

Mark's attention was in his ears when Sheila returned to the curtained cubicle.

'Must say you're a damned sight prettier than my doctor,' the patient said gallantly. Mark grimaced and Sheila bent down to whisper.

'You really mustn't talk, Mr Coventry. It sounds like a fog-horn through a stethoscope.'

'Sorry, my dear,' he whispered back, feeling self-conscious in front of a woman about the pinkness of his chest and the mat of grey fuzz down his sternum. It was such a lot of nonsense in his case, and yet he supposed many people really needed all this attention and treatment. He wondered where Beth was and if he had been missed in the Prince Edward.

Suddenly Luke's eyes widened uneasily. He couldn't believe it, but it was happening again. In one agonising writhe he was grappling with a serpent which was seeking to squeeze out his very breath and his life. Mark could hear the blocked artery beating like a drum under sandbags. He gave terse instructions for a de-coagulant to be prepared and injected. There was no time to wait or use for an ECG on a dead man.

When pain had passed and the injection was taking effect he answered the question in Luke's anxious eyes.

'You have a coronary thrombosis, Mr Coventry. We'll be keeping you in for a few days, and after that you must take things more easily.'

'My dear fellow,' Luke was aghast, 'you can't mean it. I've always believed in keeping myself fit. I do as much as any young 'un. Squash champion of my club and believe in using the old shanks's pony. I thought these coronaries happened to chaps who drove about in cars and sat on their bottoms all day long; they have fat in their arteries, don't they? You won't find an ounce of fat on me.'

'You're in very good shape for your age,' Mark admitted, 'but it might have been better for you to take up golf and leave squash to the youngsters. Walking's fine as a rule, but you may have been pushing yourself a little for some months, and arteries do harden. We're doing an electrocardiograph on you to confirm the trouble, and after that you'll be given a sedative and have a good night's sleep in a ward. Don't worry, at least you're here to hear the verdict and there's a lot we can do nowadays for your trouble. I'd better tell your wife what's happening. Naturally she's a little upset.'

'Thank you, Doctor. Good chap. You might—er—give the little woman my love, will you?'

'You'll be able to see her yourself before you go up to the ward. Just lie still and relax.'

Sheila was comforting a child nursing a thumb wrapped in a bloody bandage to its chest.

'Came downstairs for a secret feed and found Mummy's carving knife,' she explained. 'I'll need to put in a couple of stitches. I'm just telling Marie it doesn't hurt much.'

'No, not much,' he backed her up. 'What were you cutting?' he wanted to know. 'Besides your thumb,' he added.

'Bwead,' said the child. 'It was all bloody,' she confided with the dawning of satisfaction.

There was a pause when Mr Coventry had gone up to the ward and all the cubicles were cleared and empty.

'I'll warm up that coffee,' Sheila said, 'and this time you'll drink it.'

'Didn't I have some last time? That goes to show old Coventry isn't the only one tonight with a heart complaint.'

'Oh, come,' she reproved him. 'Who said hearts were involved after all this time? I seem to remember someone called Jane popping into your life as Bruce came into mine, only I waited a bit longer.'

'*And* it's still going on,' said Mark, 'which wasn't exactly obvious this afternoon, as I recall.'

'Can we cry pax or must I keep saying sorry?' she demanded.

'Consider it past history,' Mark said loftily. 'I ought to be a good loser. I'm getting quite a bit of practice.'

CHAPTER SIX

Last evening the old tramp had seen the spires of the cathedral city in the distance, but it had taken all day for him to enter its environs, for he shuffled along slowly and awkwardly nowadays, being ninety-four years of age, though he didn't know this, having lost count years ago. He had deliberately avoided main roads, not desiring to be picked up and taken care of, as kindly policemen were inclined to do with the best of intentions. They had escorted him to the Institution the night before last, not understanding his protestations because he had forgotten how to speak. The matron had said he was sick and told him not to be foolish and throw away the last of his life. Didn't they know he was sick because he was choking in that severe, green-painted ward, with its depressed patients and the scrubbed old maids who cared for them?

He had watched his clothes taken away and returned to the chair by the bed. They had been fumigated, so they said. His one thought, then, was to get out and put the scent of grass and hay and heather in them again; yes, and the sweet scent of his own sweat that helped him to know which things were his, as no man can until he knows his own smell, which God gave us in the beginning to identify us one from another.

So he had put on his clothes, reeking of a strange, nauseating disinfectant, and crept out with his bundle and his stick, three o'clock in the morning and ninety-four years old.

He had had a happy life, as he looked back, for he had lived close to the things which bring peace to a man's heart. Was there ever an unhappy tramp? He had nodded to them all from Land's End to John o' Groats, his grave, gentle, long-lived comrades; each one with the gentle heart of a child and the beard of Methuselah.

Now that he was so old memories passed before his eyes with more clarity than he saw the present. He was like an old dog which

91

knows it is soon going to die and feels an instinct to scratch itself a bed for the last time. Somewhere near here was the old dog's last bed; he could feel it in his bones, bent and rheumed as they now were.

All day the old tramp skirted the cathedral city, and as the sun sank in the summer sky he found a cemetery. He liked burial places; death has no terrors for one who has really lived. It was an old churchyard, dank and overgrown, but the grass looked soft and the spreading yews benevolent. He groaned as he settled down behind a tilted headstone, a century old. Sleep was already heavy on his eyes. He would have known the peace he sought if it hadn't been for the lovers he unwittingly disturbed. Brash, young and nervous, they told Authority about the old tramp in the graveyard.

'Anybody would think it was a ghost,' they added for good measure.

So it was that a young constable accosted the old, old man.

'Hey, dad!' It wasn't his son, he knew. They all called him that. 'You can't stay here all night.'

The tramp settled the more determinedly.

'Come on now, dad, we don't want any trouble.'

Sleep came to the old man in the middle of

this one-sided conversation and he looked so frail and dehydrated that the constable feared the worst even as he sought for signs of life. The pulse beat like a bird's. There was no more power in it than that.

★   ★   ★

'He's just old and very, very tired,' Sheila announced, watching the fading eyes close under her ministrations and smiling into them reassuringly. 'He could be a deaf-mute, which complicates matters. Traffic is a hazard to him if he can't hear it.'

There was a grumbling noise in the old tramp's throat and the eyes were open now, and indignant.

'Sorry,' she said. 'You can hear me, then?'

A sound that could have been affirmation came from him. He tried to sit up, to fold his grubby shirt over his bare chest.

'Can you tell me your name?'

The head shook imperceptibly.

'There's nothing on him to say who he is,' Sheila told Mark. 'What do we do in these cases?'

'I don't know,' Mark said thoughtfully. 'He was brought in and he's got to be logged. We'd better put him down as Mr Methuselah for hospital purposes and add in brackets "no name given".'

'Here!' Sheila said in alarm as the old man swung his legs off the bed with difficulty. 'You can't go anywhere. Not tonight, anyway,' she added quickly as the pale eyes looked alarmed. 'Maybe tomorrow, when you've had a good rest.'

There was no doubt but that the noises the tramp made were those of resistance to the idea of staying there for the night.

'Actually we've no right to keep him,' Mark said, 'if he wants to go. He wasn't doing any actual harm, was he, when he was found? He obviously prefers to sleep rough. He could be a hundred years old, easily, and he didn't get to be that age sleeping between sheets.'

'But he could go out and die somewhere.'

'He could die here, of old age, just as easily.'

They eyed one another uncertainly.

'I would want to go with him,' Sheila said, 'just to make sure he was all right.'

'Very well,' Mark granted. 'Let him sleep where he is for the night. He seems to have dropped off again, but I would sedate him if he wakes up. There seems to be a heck of a row going on out there. What's going on?'

In the reception hall Nurse Collins was in heated debate with a refined-looking elderly woman who was obviously *distraite*.

94

'Yes, Nurse?' Mark inquired. 'Is there any trouble?'

'This'—Collins looked with some hostility at the stranger before continuing—'lady returned a little while ago from Jamaica where she has been visiting her daughter and son-in-law...'

'That's right,' the woman said nervously. 'My name is Collinge—Rose Collinge—by the way, and I have been staying with Josephine, my married daughter, for two months. I returned home last Wednesday and for a couple of days I simply haven't been well. I was remarking to Nurse, here, that one can catch such terrible diseases in Jamaica, and apparently upset her.'

'No worse than anywhere else,' snapped the staff nurse, her national dander up with a vengeance. 'People shouldn't go around saying that we either smell or have worse diseases than anybody else. You can catch terrible diseases in Britain if you're unlucky.'

'Yes, well,' Sheila said soothingly, 'I think you could have a cup of coffee now, Nurse, and leave us to deal with this.'

'Poor things!' condescended Mrs Collinge as the nurse departed, stiff and erect. 'They are so sensitive.'

'If you didn't feel well,' Mark asked, 'why didn't you go to your doctor?'

'Because I told myself I was being stupid. But when I had gone to bed I felt terribly sick and faint—as though I was going to pass out. My phone didn't seem to be working, so in desperation I got the car out and came here. I—I hope I'm not being a nuisance?'

Mark nodded to Sheila to help the woman remove some clothing in the staff nurse's absence.

'Did anything untoward happen while you were visiting your daughter?' he asked a little later.

'Not really. At first I didn't like it; the spiders and other creepy-crawlies. Ugh! But I settled down and then it was really very nice. Of course Peter has a very good position and a lovely house. I wouldn't have cared to live as the natives do. Those shanty-towns are a disgrace and there are so many children! Somebody should introduce the pill.'

'Mrs Collinge, if we could forget the social problems of Jamaica for a moment, I would like to know how I can help you. When did you start feeling unwell?'

'The day after I returned I found I couldn't sleep. I blamed that on being tensed up, because I don't really like flying, and leaving Josephine for goodness knows how long. Partings do upset one. The next night I couldn't sleep again, however, and I kept seeing horrible pictures in my mind's eye.'

'What sort of things?' Mark persisted.

'Well, I saw Josephine dead and mangled—it was like a nightmare only I was awake. I thought I must be going out of my mind, or something. Then I wanted a drink of water, one time, and I saw myself get up and go to the bathroom and yet I knew I was still lying in bed. But tonight was the worst so far. I was thirsty and wanted a drink, but I just couldn't swallow. I tried and tried and finally threw it back. I felt so strange that I came here. Now, of course, I am feeling much better, which is always the way. I suppose you think I'm a stupid old woman?'

'Have you had a drink since?'

'No. Do you think it would be any trouble? Just a drink of water.'

Sheila went to get a tumbler and then watched as the woman struggled to swallow. She finally emitted the mouthful of liquid in desperation on to the floor.

'Don't worry,' Sheila said hastily. So far the symptoms Mrs Collinge evinced didn't add up to anything for her. Mark appeared to be ahead, however.

'Mrs Collinge, has your daughter a dog? Did any dog bite you while you were abroad?'

The woman paled and then laughed nervously.

'No. I don't think I would have forgotten a thing like that because I'm inclined to be timid with animals. I believe you were thinking I might have hydrophobia, Doctor, but that's impossible. I was stung several times and I did get a tiny bite on my neck.' She pointed to a healed, white scar. 'You know what did that? A bat. Not a vampire or anything like that. A fruit bat. They live in the banana plantations. One had got into my bedroom and we were all hitting out at it, horrible thing, so I suppose it felt a bit hostile and bit me as I tried to shoo it out.'

'When did this happen, Mrs Collinge?'

'About the second week I was there, about seven weeks ago. Why—?'

'That could have upset you, Mrs Collinge. We'll call our pathologist and have some tests made, but don't worry.'

Sheila followed him out of the cubicle looking alarmed.

'Mark, bats can become rabid too, can't they?'

'Yes. But we can't tell the old girl that until we're sure. She's entering the second stage of hydrophobia, in my opinion, and the sooner we put her on Pasteur's treatment, the better. We may be too late, of course. The actual bite should have been cauterised immediately, but if we tell the public all that possibly could happen to them they would never sleep soundly in their beds again. Would you call the path lab? There's always somebody on night duty. Give them the gen and tell them to get cracking.'

Within an hour Mrs Collinge's condition was confirmed and the first painfully slow injection made to counteract the poison in the system.

'Better inform her daughter by cable,' Mark advised as the woman, sedated into slumber, was taken up to a ward. 'This is bad news, but if she dies it would be worse. It's a horrible death, I believe.'

When all had been done and the department was quiet again, Sheila looked in on the old tramp. He had slipped away, however, tattered old bundle and all. Nobody had seen him go. He was too wily a bird to go out by the way he had been brought in.

'What do we do?' Sheila asked.

'Nothing. What *can* we do? Put a perfectly sensible old gent into a restrainer, like a loonie? He wanted to go and he went. Hello, who's interfered with his admittance card?'

'Not me.' Sheila looked over Mark's elbow and saw that where he had put 'Mr Methusaleh', this was now crossed out and underneath was written in wavering capitals, 'Mr J. P. Wilcox thanks all kindly.'

'The old devil!' Mark chuckled. 'He could write all the time, and there we were trying desperately to communicate with him. I bet wherever he is he's laughing.'

The old tramp was laughing. He didn't really know if he was J. P. Wilcox, but the name came most readily to his mind whenever he thought about such things. He had been delighted to find he could still write. Now he went off at a slow shuffle through quiet streets, determined to find open country before he settled down for the last time. It was summer dawn before he came to quiet woodland and sank into a ready-made bed of dried leaves. He slept all that day and all night and so death came to him, a transition from sleep to what some call oblivion, and others—heaven.

★   ★   ★

Mark called them the 'sea-bed hours', from two to four o'clock in the morning, because 'one simply can't get any lower than that'.

It was true, Sheila agreed, that at this time one was desperate for sleep and any enforced exertion seemed a terrible effort for the body to make. Also one felt depressed, as though daytime and release would never come.

'You go and have a lie-down,' Mark

suggested, watching his colleague stifle a yawn.

'No. You go if you want.'

'Shan't. Undesirable as my company may be, I refuse to leave you.'

'Nobody said your company wasn't desirable.'

'Oh. Merely less desirable than another's—is that it?'

'Mark, please don't go on!'

'Sorry. I didn't mean to go on. I was trying to pass the time with a little conversation. Would you like me to go away?'

'No—no, of course not.'

'Then allow me to take an interest in your affairs at least, if participation in them is forbidden. When—when is the great day?'

'You mean when am I getting married?'

'I did think that's what a girl called her wedding day. I may be wrong. Not experienced, you know.'

'Actually we hadn't decided on a date,' Sheila said somewhat off-handedly. 'It's absolutely ages off. My internship's the important thing on my mind at the moment.'

'Ah, yes. One presumes that you are planning to carry on working after marriage, in that case. Don't tell me he's another of us?'

'He's a doctor—yes. He's in general practice.'

'I don't know why I want to say lucky so-and-so, apart from having a girl like you, that is. Being a GP sounds so settled, somehow. This Bruce must be comfortably established. I envy him.'

'But you could be brilliant, Mark, if you find the right niche and a good sponsor, like Sir William. You shouldn't be envying anybody.'

'I'm not sure of anything nowadays, Sheila. My experiences have taught me not to count my chickens.'

'I suppose I contributed to that?'

'Not more than other things. I am suspicious of Sir William's interest in me—I don't know why. I don't feel comfortable about it, somehow. There's a hidden string I haven't spotted yet, and I'm not the stuff that makes anybody's puppet. Rather the reverse. I am inclined to be bloody-minded.'

'I have occasionally noticed,' Sheila said with a small smile.

'Yes, well ... that's the Leighton boy. Once or twice I've even been bloody-minded with Sir William, and to my surprise he hasn't shot me down in flames or booted me out. I wonder why?'

'Maybe he just likes you.'

'No, I don't think he likes me particularly. Anyway'—he shrugged—'we were talking about you. One presumes you're also heading for general practice?'

'Yes. I have no particular bent towards specialising. I did once think I'd like to take obstetrics, but I'll get my ration of that as a GP.'

'You do really love this Bruce? I mean, it isn't that you just want to be sure of marriage and your job?'

'Mark! What a thing to say!' Bruce was the more attractive to her that he offered her a ready-made job, she knew. She had never before questioned why she was so drawn to him.

'Is that an answer? A couple of outraged exclamations?'

'Mark, I don't want to discuss my affairs any longer with you.'

She had risen. He rose, too, and then did something of which he was afterwards terribly ashamed. Despite her protests he forced her arms down to her side and chased her lips, as her head turned from side to side, with the concentration of a snake hypnotising a bird. She hadn't a chance against him. He homed on those lips and feasted until she sank limply against him, making little inarticulate cries of distress and desolation. When he released her she ran off, her eyes wet, and then he knew that he had indeed found bottom in the sea-bed hours. No man could get lower. He also knew that he would always be cursed with loving the girl. Surely that was punishment enough?

Sheila had found refuge in the linen cupboard and there she sought to calm herself and ponder the situation which had arisen. She was not angry with Mark; it was as natural for the elements they both were to fuse together as it was for lightning to home into earth, no matter what was damaged on the way. The fact that other things were in the way was the one which had to be faced, the situation dealt with. She had discovered she couldn't bear to discuss with Mark her plans to marry anyone else. Each word was a sword-thrust towards self-destruction. Every time she saw Mark her plans with Bruce appeared more shabby and opportunist. It wasn't enough for her and certainly not sufficient to offer Bruce: he was a good man and inclined to be a lonely one, but loneliness is often preferable to a grudging companionship.

She heard footsteps in the corridor outside. They might be looking for her, and it would never do to be caught huddling away in the dark like a frightened child. She blew her nose, squared her shoulders and sailed forth. Mark eyed her anxiously as she reappeared in the main Casualty station, but she looked serene and businesslike and returned his gaze unfalteringly. It is sometimes a relief even to have made up one's mind to an action before the business of carrying it out. Mark thought, 'She must be hating my guts, but she's trying not to show it. I mustn't allow that sort of thing to happen again between us. She told me to get off the grass, and by golly I'll stay off. I didn't think I could be so ruddy weak. Of course she has her life to live as she sees best and it's up to me to be a good loser. But oh, God, I wish this blessed night was over! I didn't imagine that one hour of sheer despair could seem so long. How can I see her and not show that I'm still mad about her? I can put on an act, I suppose ... pretend I was just playing the damned fool. We can't just stand and stare at each other.'

'Hello!' said Mark, forcing a brazen smile. 'I suppose I should say I'm sorry, but at half-past two a.m. one will do just anything to enliven the drag. That was the most entertaining way I could think of, but if you didn't want to play you could have screamed, or something. Running off as though you were outraged was a bit naîve for a grown woman.'

It was now, however, that Sheila felt a sense of outrage. Forced to look at things at point-blank range and see all the flaws in her plans, and now have it revealed that something she had taken quite seriously was a bit of masculine gambolling made her see red.

'I didn't scream,' she told him, 'because I couldn't for—for you, you brute. But just try something like that again and I'll react as I think fit. I'm not one of your little nurse friends, put here for your casual entertainment. Just remember that in future.'

'The answer to that seems to be hoity-toity,' said Mark with a shrug. 'Don't imagine I have to plead for any woman's favours.'

'Even the weather has changed,' was his snide remark before they parted, hostility crackling between them.

'The weather can be depended on to be variable,' Sheila retorted. 'One imagines people will be different, but they rarely are.'

'Good luck to Bruce from me, when you're next in touch,' he said brightly. 'The poor devil's going to need it!'

'We don't need your blessing, fortunately,' she returned, and lowered her eyes as Staff Nurse Collins passed on her way to hand over to her opposite number on the day staff.

'Brawling like that, in public,' she thought grimly as she went off towards the dining-room, determined not to be thought off her food by the arrogant Mr Leighton. 'Whatever is happening to me?'

She knew the answer, of course. Within the

past forty-eight hours her deepest emotions had surprisingly surfaced and informed her that most of the time she was only half alive. It is always amazing how contented we are with our lot until something happens or someone tells us there is much more to be had, then by our very nature we find we cannot live without it. But Mark, who had dangled the apple, had only been playing with her.

Now Sheila had to face more unsavoury facts: even though Mark had not been serious in arousing her interest in him again, could she honestly carry on with Bruce as though nothing had happened? Should she at this moment be thankful that she had Bruce to turn back to?

Here, in the dining-room, day and night staffs overlapped. Sheila could hear Mark greeting Martha Haley in familiar tones.

'Hello, old thing! I believe we have a date this afternoon?'

'Yes, we have. Sleep tight until then. I'll need your absolute concentration while you're with me.'

Some young bloods who overheard this gave loud wolf-whistles which brought a quick, bright smile from Miss Haley.

Sheila was saying a little prayer, asking for guidance, under her breath. How could she possibly hurt Bruce, who was innocent? Yet how could she not hurt him in the long run whatever she decided?

Though she believed in prayer, in a vague sort of way, she didn't expect an answer quite as soon or directly. The dining-room supervisor called for silence and asked if Dr Devaney was present.

Sheila rose, looking mystified.

'You're wanted on the phone, Doctor.'

The staff were not encouraged to receive outside calls except in emergency, but Sheila was directed into Sister Outpatients' office without comment. It was Bruce on the line, and she almost fainted.

'Is anything wrong?' she quavered.

'I don't know, my sweet. I found I couldn't sleep last night and my first thought this morning was, I won't write Sheila, I'll phone. I don't think I'm the psychic type, but anyhow it's nice to hear your voice.'

She forced herself to take advantage of this coincidence. It would have been much easier to gossip the time away and put things off till another day.

'Bruce, you *must* be psychic. I desperately want to see you urgently.'

'Oh?' There was a pause. She could imagine him chewing his moustache and pondering this somewhat hysterical outburst.

'I'm just off duty, as you'll have guessed,'

she said more calmly, 'but if I have a few hours in bed I could meet you somewhere between here and Devon during the afternoon. Would that be possible?'

'It really is urgent, then?' he asked quietly.

'Yes. Yes, it is.'

'Must it be today?'

'I would appreciate seeing you today. If you'd still been at home I could have caught the fast train at midday and been with you in an hour. Devon's rather far off, though.'

'They have fast trains from Devon too, Sheila. Now listen carefully. I want you to take a pill and get your sleep. I'll come all the way to see you. It isn't a very good day for fishing in any case. I'll come and ask for you when I arrive, and we'll go and have a high tea somewhere and chat.'

'I—I do appreciate your gesture, Bruce. But then you always are so very nice.'

'Yes,' he laughed, and said surprisingly, 'but the nice chap never has the advantage, somehow. Perhaps he's too nice to take it. Well, pop off into bed, now, my dear. I'll be seeing you later.'

She felt dazed as she replaced the receiver, as though she was taking part in some play written without her knowledge and having a conclusion hidden in terrifying mystery. She went to the RMO and asked if she might have a sleeping capsule.

'At your age?' he smiled. 'First night duty, eh? When you've been in the game as long as I have, Doctor, you'll be able to sleep standing up on your feet at any time and in any place. Anyhow'—he handed over a cellophane packet containing a capsule—'here you are. Don't make a habit of it.'

Having been in touch with Bruce had somehow relaxed her, and half an hour after taking the capsule she was sleeping like the dead.

CHAPTER SEVEN

Mark, who had not taken a sleeping capsule and had slept for a couple of hours like a drunk with a hangover, awakened feeling like one with a thick head and a furred tongue.

'Physician, heal thyself,' he told the mirror on the wall of his room. 'If they can't have bread let them eat cake, and if I can't have Sheila I'll have Martha, whether I damned well like it or not. She's a woman, isn't she? She does all the right things in the right places, and sooner or later I've got to react normally to somebody else. The sooner, I say, the better.'

By three o'clock he was at the gate. 'At milady's service,' he said, mock deferentially, as Martha drew up in the MG, and slid over for him to drive. He glanced at her in a way which told her that even for a beautiful woman she had more than come up to expectations. She was wearing a suit of green silk jersey and her dark hair was controlled by a cleverly tied transparent scarf. She was used to admiring glances, but revelled particularly in Mark's. It was the first time he had looked at her like that and she felt that the time spent on her preparations for this outing was reaping its reward. At times she had resented his stubbornness in resisting her almost open invitations to have an affair with her. She had always needed masculine attention and admiration, but now she felt the urge to make an admirer into a husband. Even the most beautiful and attractive of women is called a spinster after a certain age and, unjustified though it may be, the title has the ring of failure about it among one's married friends and acquaintances.

The rain had ceased by midday and now the sun shone from a windblown sky.

'Let's go and buy my car first,' said Martha, her low voice heavy with significance.

'First?' echoed Mark, giving her another of those assessing glances. 'Have we a

111

programme, then?'

'Leave all that to me. For your services as my advisor you must be suitably rewarded.'

'You know I said I would like to buy this car? How about it?'

'I may give it to you if you're good.'

'No, seriously,' he said quite sharply. 'Don't let's mix business with pleasure. How much?'

She had been quite serious when she said he could have the car. He would have to pay for it in coin of her choosing, of course, but it was a way of putting him into her debt which should have attracted him by the rules she observed.

'Mark, I don't need money from you,' she said in honeyed tones. 'You have the use of the car and welcome. They always do you with this part-exchange lark in any case.'

'Martha, I want to *buy* a car. I have money in the bank for that purpose. I wouldn't dream of accepting my registrar's cast-off model as a gift even if he were a man. But as it is—'

'You don't accept gifts from women. Is that it?'

'That *is it*,' he said with emphasis. 'A car isn't like a tie-pin or a box of hankies. It's the subject of a deal between interested parties. Now, do you want to sell privately or not?'

'If you want it, Mark, I'll sell it to you. I

don't know about the price. I have absolutely no idea.' She liked this aggressive masculinity of his. He was poor and proud and a novelty.

'Very well, we'll get it valued by a dealer right now and whatever he offers I'll pay you two hundred pounds more. That should cover any profit he would allow himself for a re-sale. OK?'

'If you say so, Mark.' She was enjoying her role of the little woman bowing before male superiority and knowledge.

They had the car valued twice. The first time the offered price was ridiculous in Mark's opinion, as was proved when the dealer raised it by a hundred pounds when he could see the couple were determined to try elsewhere. The second dealer offered what Mark thought was a very fair price.

'Right. My offer of an extra two hundred still stands,' said Mark to Martha as they drove away to consider. 'I can write you a cheque when we get back.'

'OK,' she agreed. 'Now you have a car and poor Martha hasn't. Let's go and buy my beautiful Porsche.'

It was a lovely car, dark blue with grey upholstery and a mahogany instrument-panel—things Martha noticed—and with a sound engine and chassis and new tyres, which Mark looked for. They went for a spin in the new car and it was like riding on velvet.

'Well?' Martha asked. 'Shall I buy it?'

'Yes. It's a beaut,' Mark agreed, 'but knock him down a few hundred. There isn't a queue of likely purchasers. You can afford to hum and ha a little, get him nervous.'

'Oh, you are clever!' Martha smiled admiringly. 'I saw this car, fell in love with it and I would have paid whatever was asked without argument. I suppose that's the trouble with always having had too much money.'

'What an enviable affliction! I hope it's catching,' Mark smiled his lopsided smile.

Not only was a bit of haggling expected, but Martha finally paid less than she had anticipated for the Porsche, and delivery was promised next day at the hospital. She wrote a cheque there and then and looked pleased with her new toy.

'Why does a girl like you want an expensive car?' Mark asked. 'Don't your men friends— legion they must be—take you about in theirs?'

'I haven't so many men friends as you imagine, Mark dear, and a girl has to get about. I never think of using buses or trains. You probably think I'm spoilt.'

'Why should success spoil one? You have a good job and deserve to reap the benefits.'

'Oh, I couldn't live on my salary as a doctor. I've always had a private allowance from my father. I like my work. I think people go to rot who don't have a serious occupation. My father is Professor Haley of the Clinic.'

'I had suspected there must be a connection. I never dreamt I would one day be sitting alongside Professor Haley's daughter like this.'

'You must come and meet Daddy one day. Would you like that?'

'Would I!' was Mark's heartfelt exclamation. He thought how happy he could be today if it wasn't for one secret, nagging ache dragging his spirits down. He was with a pretty woman who confessed to being the daughter of an eminent surgeon whose name was almost as regularly quoted in that field as Lister's was in his. He had also almost acquired a car at long last and could still feel fairly solvent, again at long last. There was so much to the oyster that was his world and yet he was denied the love of his life. Of course things wouldn't have worked out with Jane; she had been the best of pals, but there hadn't been much softness about her. He couldn't imagine Jane trembling within his arms like a trapped bird; Jane, not wishing to co-operate in such a venture, would have had him on the floor in a flash—she was a Judo expert—or

115

have brought up her knee and kicked where it hurt. Jane wasn't exactly tiny and feminine; she was a healthy Amazon, for which many of her patients were extremely thankful. But Sheila ... now there was a dainty miss who roused every masculine urge to a screaming crescendo. No wonder somebody else had fallen in love with her.

When she had confronted him in Casualty that first night—was it really less than three days ago?—he had felt as though a mule had kicked him, though he hoped it didn't show. He had never forgotten Sheila, but when polio had struck, with its threat of permanent invalidism, he hadn't felt like chasing after a girl who must be doing very well without him and playing on her sympathies to take him back again. When sufficient time has passed all grief loses its raw edges. He thought he had got over Sheila when Jane came along. Perhaps Jane knew he hadn't, that there was a secret place in his heart where no one was welcome to trespass. But she had apparently successfully got over him. She had been tempted to step back into the past for only a few entranced moments, but her future was apparently more to her liking. She had said, 'I don't want to go on—with you. I can't.' Last night's little fracas had been his desperate argument against her decision. He had learned that you can't use force on a woman to make her change her mind. He had never been a cad in all his life before. It had left a bad taste in his mouth.

He had tried to play up to what he imagined was Martha's expectation of him, being hard and bright and sophisticated, but he didn't quite understand her in her present mood. She was his boss, after all, and yet she was rather rubbing in the 'What a big, strong, clever man you are!' sort of thing while bringing attention to her own inadequacies.

Since they had left the garage showrooms she had been back at the wheel of the MG.

'Where are we going?' he asked suddenly, coming out of his reverie. 'This isn't the way back to the hospital.'

'I have no intention of going back yet. We're going to my place to relax.'

'Your place?' he echoed. He thought she meant the family home and felt somewhat dismayed at the prospect of meeting her parents with so little warning. 'I didn't know you lived hereabouts.'

'I have a flat. I keep it, even though I'm in residence at the hospital, because it's so nice to get away from the place sometimes and if one has friends, well'—she shrugged— 'everything is so public at St John's.'

They drew up outside a handsome Georgian

house in a row of such houses. The small front garden was neatly kept, with chain-link fencing painted white.

'I'm on the first floor,' Martha announced. 'There's a staircase at the side.'

It was a very handsome flat with a large sitting-room, a kitchen and dining area combined and a big bedroom with a bathroom leading off. Mark shrank from the sight of the large white satin expanse of bed with a curtained tester over the head drawn into an expensive-looking coronet. It was all very feminine and extravagant. He wondered what he was doing there.

Martha played hostess and made some tea. She had taken off her head-scarf and her dark hair fell freely.

'I have to work tonight, you know,' he reminded her.

'I know. You poor darling, you must be worn out. I know—I'll show you some photographs and that will send you to sleep for an hour. Looking at other people's snapshot albums always does. I'll get you back in good time, so don't worry.'

She sat beside him on the large sofa, curled her legs under her and began showing him pictures of Martha at all stages; she had even been a beautiful child or else had taken care to see that only flattering snaps had been kept.

After ten minutes he yawned uninhibitedly and smiled at her.

'Not bored, honestly. Just tired.'

'Here, make yourself comfy.' She pulled his head down to her shoulder. 'I've heard it said that one can only sleep in the company of friends. See what that makes me!'

He not only slept. He dreamt that he was kissing Sheila again and didn't want to wake up. Wake he did, however. He looked round in amazement and wondered where he could be. He remembered and saw that it was after eight o'clock. Martha was no longer beside him. He wanted to freshen up, to go back to the hospital.

'Martha!' he called tentatively. When she didn't answer he rose and looked around. She wasn't in the kitchen. The bedroom door was wide open and in horror he realised that he was seeing Martha Haley in a state of undress. She was standing with her back to him wearing a pair of black lace briefs and a bra. Even while he watched the bra came off, revealing the long expanse of ivory which was her back. Quickly as he stepped aside he felt terrible, like an intruder. Why couldn't the stupid woman have closed the door?

'Martha!' he called again. 'Is it all right if I sluice my face in the kitchen?'

'Come and have a quick shower in the

bathroom,' she called. 'You'll feel much better for it.'

'Right-ho,' he agreed, giving her another minute to either don a robe or a dress. When he entered the bedroom, however, she was still in underclothes, though they were now white. He resolutely averted his eyes and went into the bathroom, pointedly closing the door between them. While the shower was running, however, she opened the door and collected his clothes, taking them out with her.

'They get soaked,' she called in explanation. 'I know from experience.'

When he had finished showering he knew a moment of panic. Did one call out like a nervous schoolgirl, 'May I have my clothes, please?' or enter the bedroom wearing only a towel? He decided on the latter course; Martha was still semi-nude and obviously not worrying about it.

'I'll put some togs on if you'll tell me where they are,' he pronounced.

'You have lovely shoulders, Mark,' she told him admiringly.

'Thanks. But I like them covered when I'm with a lady. Now—'

'Oh, don't be so shy, Mark. And I'm not a lady at this moment, I'm a woman with a very attractive man.'

She had approached, to his consternation, and stood as though for his delectation revealing her bare midriff and long, slim thighs.

'I'm not ashamed of being a woman,' she pouted at him.

He began to get the message at last. She had brought him here wanting him to start love-play, or worse. He felt trapped and rather ridiculous, in only a towel.

'Look, Martha,' he urged, 'tell me where I can find my clothes. This thing's not only slipping, it's damp.'

'I will if you do what you did before. I liked it.'

'What did I do before?' he asked, mystified.

'You kissed me when you were pretending to be asleep.'

He opened his mouth to gasp a denial, but she mistook the gesture and fastened her lips to his like a limpet. He felt her against him with a sense of deep revulsion, knowing that she was experienced in such things and trying to tar him with the same brush.

'Now I'll get your clothes,' she told him. Her hips swayed as she crossed the room to a closet. He had never seen anything so blatant or anyone more brazen. 'There!' she threw his things on the bed. 'I just want to show you something absolutely gorgeous.'

While she was behind a padded-silk screen he leapt into his jeans and shirt with a sense of relief and release. He was back in the living-room when Martha reappeared. This time she was wearing a diaphanous white negligée with a froth of frills and ribbons.

'There!' she said. 'Don't you just love me in this?'

Once more he was speechless.

'Cat got your tongue, Mark?' she teased him.

He swallowed and closed his eyes.

'You know where I live now, darling,' she said huskily. 'I know how you feel, but this isn't quite the right time, is it? Not with you having to rush off.'

He found speech.

'You can't know how I feel,' he said harshly.

'Oh, but, darling—'

'I'm not your darling, and I feel sick at the way you're exposing yourself,' he said gruffly. 'For God's sake put on some clothes and stop playing around!'

She paused and regarded him.

'Just because you have to work there's no need to suppress your natural feelings,' she said archly. 'Ever since you kissed me I've known what you wanted.'

'I did not knowingly kiss you,' he corrected

122

her, 'though the way you've been hanging round my neck it has been almost impossible to avoid you. I do not want to kiss you. Neither do I believe you have any intention of allowing anybody to play the fool with you. You like to tease and lead men on, but I should imagine there's quite a high price-tag on your favours. I do not happen to be in the bidding, however, so forget it.'

Now her eyes were cat-like, watchful.

'Are you serious?' she asked.

'Yes, Martha, I'm serious. I'm sorry if I led you to think otherwise.'

She seized on this remark to transfer the blame for her present discomfiture.

'Yes, you did rather lead me to think otherwise,' she hissed. 'I think it's despicable when a man comes to a woman's flat and pretends he's just come for tea. You'd better get out.' Her voice shrilled. 'Get out!'

'Very well. You're sure I can't drop you anywhere?'

'You dropped me a moment ago, if you remember? In any case, I can drop myself anywhere I care to go. I still have my old car outside. You don't think you're getting it now, do you?'

'Oh, I see. Then I'll wish you goodnight.'

'Don't think you've heard the last of this, Mr Leighton. I don't forget or forgive very easily.'

'You fortunately have little to forgive.'

He ran down the staircase outside, glad to gulp in the fresh air again. How many others had been led through the ritual of the open bedroom door and the strip-tease within? he wondered. She must have been aware that she was observed. Every movement had been so casual and studied. Martha—his boss. He just couldn't believe it. Whenever he saw her in the hospital, white-coated and cool, he would remember her abandoned flaunting in that negligée.

Sheila . . . Sheila would never show herself off like that. Sheila was shy and yet he well knew the fires that could blaze within her, but they were disciplined fires that could be banked at will. How lovely it would be to burn with Sheila on the pyre of love's fulfilment!

CHAPTER EIGHT

Tilly, the corridor maid, tapped gently, opened the door of number four on which was displayed a card bearing the legend DO NOT DISTURB, poked her head round and was rewarded by a protestingly turned fair head.

'Oh, Doctor!' greeted Tilly. 'I thought you

would like to know it's after five and there's a gentleman been asking for you . . .'

'Oh!' Remembrance and realisation came to Sheila Devaney in that one exclamation.

'He did say you were not to be woken up special, though,' Tilly went on. 'But that was an hour ago. He said he'd be in the sitting-room and I passed the word to Moira to see he got a cup of tea.'

'Very kind of you, Tilly. I'll get up now.'

She felt self-conscious confronting Bruce a little later. There was another couple in the sitting-room, so she felt grateful that he did not rush over and embrace her. She had to admit to herself, however, that it was unlikely he would have done so had they been alone. She had often found it was she who made the initial, affectionate advances.

'So you came?' she asked unnecessarily. 'What must you be thinking of me?'

'When I saw this place I thought you must be a heroine, my dear. It's so huge and must be infernally busy.'

'You haven't seen St John's before, then?'

'No. I haven't exactly been everywhere.'

'Would you like to look round?'

'Why not? See how the other half lives, eh?'

Bruce was a very interested observer of all they saw, which included the geriatric unit and the maternity department; he was most

125

impressed by the Medical Sciences wing and all the apparatus at the students' disposal.

'They've come on since my day,' he had to admit, and she realised that in fifteen years medicine had taken leaps and bounds forward over the barriers of knowledge. He was really a generation behind her in techniques, though doubtless he kept up with his reading and maybe they would have had many arguments had they married and worked together as planned.

As they came back through the hospital corridors a young, dark nurse came out of a linen closet wiping her eyes. Sheila looked up, for nobody liked to be observed indulging in a private weep. This reminded the young doctor that not only she had troubles. Everybody, at some time, wept, or wanted to.

Bruce said, 'You wanted to talk to me. Where shall we go?'

'Did you mean that about high tea?'

'Not necessarily. I had a good lunch on the train and tea and biscuits brought me in the hospital.'

'Oh. Well, there's a park quite near. It isn't far and I know all the short cuts nowadays.'

They secured a bench in a quiet corner overlooking a cricket pitch. As there was no game being played there were not many people around.

'Would you like to light your pipe?' Sheila asked.

'Would you like me to?'

'Please. It will keep the midges away.'

She knew, miserably, that she had played for time long enough. Bruce was being very patient, but he must also be curious as to why she had summoned him so summarily. She put this question into nervous words.

'You—you must be wondering what this is all about, Bruce?'

'Yes, I do. I've already concluded that it's something to do with our personal arrangement.'

'Oh? How did you guess?'

'Sheila!' he said in fond exasperation. 'I'm not an ass. If the trouble was to do with a third party, such as somebody doing you down professionally or insulting you or even physically assaulting you, then you would have told me over the phone and I would have come, to offer you comfort or advice. But when I had to come, in such haste, and you offered no explanation, I could only think of one thing. I think it's best to face the worst, then one can only be relieved if it's a lesser evil.'

'And what did you think was the worst thing that could happen, Bruce?'

'I told myself you had fallen in love with

somebody else, Sheila. Was I right?'

She seemed to deflate in front of his eyes. In a way it was a relief to have him put it into words.

'Yes and no, Bruce,' she told him quietly. 'I think I always have been in love with Mark. I have mentioned Mark to you previously?'

'Yes, you have. But you can't live in the past, Sheila. First love is always rather unique. After that we have to take the less exciting stuff which nevertheless is inclined to endure.'

She thought about this statement and then explained.

'Bruce, I don't think I've made the situation clear to you. Mark isn't the past any longer. He's here at St John's and we—we're on duty together in Casualty all this week.'

Bruce seemed to withdraw and freeze a little.

'I see,' he said, 'and now you're going to tell me something has happened in the face of created opportunity?'

She blushed as this registered.

'Oh, Bruce! What do you think I am? Nothing has happened. At least, everything and—and nothing. I know I'm still in love with Mark, but he doesn't feel the same about me. I simply felt it wasn't fair to go on with you, knowing my feelings. I must confess I thought of doing just that—but I couldn't.'

'I see.' The pipe-smoke was emitted in quick puffs. This always meant Bruce was agitated. 'But surely this fellow's interest can be re-aroused when he knows you're free?'

'Oh, Bruce, I don't think so. Frankly he has gone down in my estimation and I wish I wasn't in love with him. But there it is.'

'I take it you want to be free of me?'

'Oh, Bruce!' she gave a little sob. 'What a way to put it! I don't think I do, frankly, but I had to tell you what has happened—or rather, not happened. If you still want me to go on, then . . .'

He said, considering his words carefully, 'No, Sheila, I don't think we could ever go on after this. I would obviously interpret every marital criticism of yours into expressions of longing and regret for another. You would no doubt see in my periodic irritation a determination to spite you for having admitted you're not in love with me wholeheartedly. A relationship which can't be wholly natural, which hesitates to tread for fear of being misunderstood, is not for you and me. Perhaps I do understand how you feel more than you imagine. When I was a student I, too, fell deeply in love with the daughter of one of my tutors. I never told you about her because it was never a partnership. She knew nothing of my feelings. To me they were new and sacred and unrepeatable; the only satisfaction. I knew joy in seeing her occasionally and I walked miles just to gaze on the house which was a shrine because of my goddess. Stupid, you think. Old Bruce, cockeyed with love. I thought so, too, for many years, but when I saw the show *My Fair Lady*, and they sang that song, "On the street where you live", it was Julia I thought of, not you, and I also remembered, with some pangs, how it had felt to be hopelessly in love with her.'

Sheila tried not to feel hurt. 'So we're each well shot of the other,' she murmured.

'No, we're not. It would have been good, and you know it. But I'm no longer a hopeless, passionate young man. I've often thought I was too old and set for you, but you seemed so mature at times. You're just being your age at the moment, Sheila, and nobody can blame you. I don't. I only wish I could jog this fellow's arm a bit.'

'Oh, no, Bruce, I couldn't bear that. I— suppose you should have this back?' She handed over the ring. She suddenly felt naked without it, as though she was swimming in deep sea without a lifebelt.

'Yes, I'd better.' He put it in his pocket with his loose change and she felt it would be lost quite soon and unregretted. She also felt it was no longer any business of hers to fidget about its safety. Bruce wouldn't be rushing to get engaged to anybody else. He had already been quite comfortable in his bachelorhood when they first met. 'Well, can I be any more help, Sheila, or shall I go now?'

'Where are you going, Bruce?'

'Oh, back to Devon to finish my holiday. Are you disappointed that I haven't cracked up?' His smile twisted a little on his face. 'Don't think I don't mind, Sheila. I do. But I don't think I ever quite believed there would be any happy-ever-after in our case. That's why I'm not too surprised by all this. You—won't want to keep in touch?'

'No,' she said with an ache in her throat. 'I don't want us to become too casual, and that's what happens.'

'Then I'll say goodbye now, and wish you well.'

'Goodbye, Bruce.' They shook hands and hers emerged mangled from the contact.

'Shall I walk you back to the hospital?' he asked formally.

'No. The station's over there. You can get a taxi outside the main park gates. I'll stroll back slowly.'

They each turned away and Sheila deliberately didn't look back for ages. When

131

she did essay a glance there was no sign of
Bruce and that episode was quite over. She
began to sob in a dry, racked way which
brought no relief. She felt as thought she had
lost a limb.

★　　　★　　　★

Love was at the bottom of May Kingston's
trouble, also; love that had been desperate and
not stopped to reason or consider the
consequences. Now, at nineteen, and a
second-year probationer attached to a general
medical ward at St John's Hospital, she knew
for certain that she was pregnant. She was sick
every morning now, and it was getting more
difficult to hide from her companions. That
morning the comedienne of her set, Cunliffe,
had wagged an admonitory finger and asked,
'Hello, and what have you been up to when
you were supposed to be studying for your
Materia Medica?' The other girls had laughed
and she had said quickly, 'It's summer
tummy. I always get it.'

But she knew what it was all right; there
were other signs and symptoms and she had
read them all up in her copy of *Home Nursing*.
She was pregnant, and Bernie Hull, a medical
student and her husband of five months, was
responsible. They hadn't meant to get married

132

when they first met; they really liked and respected each other and their studies. It was only after a party when they had both had a little too much to drink that the other thing roared like a dragon when they were near each other, an urgency to touch, to embrace, to get closer than close. Yet they were not loose people; May had been brought up to respect the tenets taught in Chapel and Bernie was a Jew. To try to tell their parents about this fatal attraction was a lost cause from the start, and they knew it, and yet they were also convinced that such love could never be again and it was theirs to either take or throw away.

'So we nip up to Scotland and get married,' Bernie said after their fourth passionate meeting, holding on to his self-control only because there was the promise and he was convinced, as his father had assured him, that marriage glorified the act he was now constantly contemplating. This girl was the only female he could see in a forest of females, with her short, dark hair in a bob and her brown eyes and the soft plumpness of rounded cheeks. She could pass for a Jewish girl, Bernie assured himself, looking to the time when his parents would have to know. But for the moment he had to possess her and get the madness out of his system which was interfering with his studies. They both took their annual leave in Scotland and there they married; somehow all was a bit of an anti-climax thereafter, however. May, from being a siren, became a somewhat peevish and disappointed bride. 'Is that *all*?' she would ask querulously. 'Well, I needn't have bothered!' From being the torch which had lit his passions she had deteriorated into a somewhat damp squib. She liked her secret marital status, but even this palled when she was not allowed to tell anybody.

'I'll get kicked out, then you,' Bernie warned her grimly. 'Then where will we be?'

Where, indeed!

As a student nurse May was not allowed to marry. Neither were medical students encouraged to take such steps while they were in training. If they were married already and could persuade their wives to co-exist on their meagre grants, then that was their look-out. There was a fool born every minute, so it was said.

May thought that it was unkind fate which had done this thing to her, who didn't even enjoy the intimacy of married life. She was dutiful, of course, but she expected Bernie to take care. She had just read a story in one of her favourite magazines about a young wife who discovered she was going to have a baby. That one had thought it was a kind of poetry, a living seed planted within her and nurtured in love. May didn't think poetical thoughts. She unashamedly panicked.

'Whatever am I going to do?' she asked when the morning's nausea had passed off, leaving her feeling weak and drained.

Bernie, when he knew, was as aghast as she was.

'Oh, my God!' he cried. 'You can't be pregnant! How can you be sure?'

May had grown faintly hostile.

'I've waited over two months to be sure,' she told him sharply. 'I don't want to believe it either, but there it is. If I wait long enough everybody'll be able to tell. This is a hospital full of would-be midwives who notice little things like that.'

'Heck, May,' he said grumpily, 'I thought you'd have watched out for this sort of thing.'

'Me watch out?' she shrilled. 'Why not you? Anybody'd think I made this baby on my own.'

'Shut up! D'you want everybody to hear?'

He wondered if Romeo and Juliet would have reached posterity if they had succeeded in getting together. After five months all the glitter had gone; this girl-wife of his had a round fat face, and with a fat body she would look awful.

'Heck!' he said again.

135

'Don't keep saying that, Bernie. Tell me what I must do.'

'Must do. Must do,' he echoed. 'Well, at least we're married,' he tried for starters.

'I know that. But I can't have this baby. I'd lose my job. You're nearly a doctor and you must tell me what to do.'

Her meaning sank home and he jumped up excitedly.

'Oh no!' he said. 'Oh, no. We're not taking any risks of that sort. One of our senior students was kicked out last year for helping some woman dispose of her mistake, and now he's out of the profession for life. Six wasted years—think of that! And I'm not nearly a doctor. I have four years of studies still ahead providing I pass all my exams, and the more I learn the less I seem to know. What a laugh, to get one's wife pregnant and a birth-control clinic right here under our noses.'

'You're just trying to make me feel guilty,' May whimpered. 'You don't know how sick I am, how I'd give anything for this not to have happened, how I cry every night.'

'Oh, May,' he tried to love her, went through the motions. 'You're not to cry. It's a natural happening, after all.'

'Yes, but it's not happening to you, is it? They say a confinement's awful and you forget the pains only because you'd never have any more children if you could remember them. And where would I go to have it? My mum would turn white, I can tell you. I live in a small town and nobody would believe I was married when it happened. My parents would be finished, and they don't have much as it is; the Chapel, a few socials, and my dad plays the organ a bit. He—he isn't strong, either, and knowing I was married to you would probably kill him.'

'You know something, baby? My father would wail for a week if he knew I'd married a Gentile. I can't run to him for help. We're in a mess whichever way you look at it.'

'Then tell me how to get out of it.'

'You won't be having this kid tomorrow,' Bernie snapped, 'so I'll have to think things out. Try not to worry.'

'That's asking a lot. I *am* worried. I wish I could die this minute.'

'Don't be a stupid little fool!'

They parted thus, in anger, the precious experience between them now grown into something horrid, like malignancy. For a week, each day growing more desperate, May heard not one word from Bernie. She began to think he had deserted her and then a letter arrived from him.

'... I've just heard of a third-year nurse who got herself pregnant and "confessed" to

Matron. They sent her somewhere to have the kid and get it adopted and took her back like a shot. She's a Sister now, in another hospital. Apparently one does better with the authorities as a fallen woman than if one breaks the rules and gets married. I think this is our way out, May. You'd better go to Matron and tell her you're in trouble, cry and play on her heart-strings a bit, but don't mention that it was me, and after you're back working again we'll just have to be jolly careful. You'll simply have to pretend to join the legion of unmarried mothers for both our sakes. Also, to make it more believable, I don't think we'd better meet for a bit. You always know where to find me . . .'

May read the letter again and felt sick. Did Bernie know what it would be like to live with people like Cunliffe whose meat and drink was other people's indiscretions? Cunliffe with her mimicry of a pregnant woman trying to tie her shoelaces; and her mock-hearty imitation of Matron, 'Well? How is our little mother-to-be today? Sick as a dog? Good! Good! I knew you'd be fine.'

'I'll kill myself first,' said May in desperation.

All day May was in a tizzy of apprehension and fear. She was constantly in trouble with Sister and could do nothing right. It was a relief when she was told to put the fresh linen away and she could shut herself in the linen closet to have a good cry. When she emerged a woman doctor accompanied by a man was passing, and she looked away quickly, hoping they couldn't tell she had been weeping. All she had, it appeared, was a choice of evils, and Bernie's idea was the worst of all. Her only comfort was that she *was* married, that the baby *wouldn't* bear the stigma of illegitimacy when it arrived.

She should have finished her spell of duty at five-thirty, but Sister was in one of her vindictive moods.

'Nurse Kingston, there are three patients who have not been bathed, as you well know.'

'Yes, Sister. They were expecting to be visited by Dr Rydal.'

'He is obviously not coming now, Nurse. I like all my patients bathed and clean and no backlog of work left for tomorrow. The laggard nurse never catches up. I suggest you bed-bath Mrs Addams, Mrs Keel and Miss Foggarty before you go off duty.'

'But, Sister—'

'Yes, Nurse?' The voice was forbidding, on the *qui vive* for the lame excuse.

'Only that I'm not feeling very well, Sister.'

'Oh?' the gimlet eyes raked the other. How pretty some of these girls were with their smooth cheeks and shining hair. Why had they all to be so lazy with it? 'What seems to be the trouble?'

'My stomach, Sister. It's upset.'

'Oh, that's too bad. Well, you run along to see Dr Allinson, and if he says you're sick enough you may be excused duty.'

May quickly backed down. 'Well, actually, Sister, I am feeling a bit better. Perhaps I could do the bed-baths.'

'Well, that *is* up to you, Nurse. Nobody is asked to work here who is ill, and that's what we employ a special staff physician for. Dr Allinson knows his job and that a sick nurse is an inefficient nurse. I shall leave it entirely to you to decide.'

'I'll stay on duty, Sister.'

'Right. I shall be along to help you shortly.'

The sad part of all this was that May was genuinely not feeling fit. Apart from her morning sickness she had spent a long hard day on her feet and was feeling particularly exhausted. The idea of turning three heavy, helpless women while she bathed them made her cringe, and Sister's offer of help she knew was merely optimistic. The two nurses on late duty were feverishly busy about their own routine, so May had to fill the heavy water jugs, put them on the trolley, trundle this down the ward, prepare the patient's bed, wrap the patient in special blankets, look out her own towels and soap and start at the top, then the bottom, thirdly the middle and finally the patient's back which it was most important should be kept clean and chafe-free in the bedridden. All this May did three times on her own. Sister arrived just as she was turning the third woman, Miss Foggarty, who was as large and heavy as a horse.

'Oh-er!' gasped May. 'Oh-er!'

'Nurse?' questioned Sister. 'Is it your stomach again? You've gone quite pale.'

'Oh, I'll be all right. I twisted myself, Sister.'

'How many times have I said not to try to lift patients alone, Nurse? Tell me how many times? I think you had better run along now. You can manage the trolley? Good! I'll give Miss Foggarty a little rub with spirit and straighten her bed.'

May pondered on the pain which had appeared to rip her pelvis apart for a moment back there. Could it be a twisted muscle? It had gone now, but she was so tired she would cut supper and go straight to bed. She shared a room with three other second-year nurses, including Cunliffe, but only Margaret West was there when she arrived and began to undress.

'What kept you?' asked Margaret.

'Three bed-baths. One of these days I shall kill Sister Gibson!'

This was loose talk. There were few popular Ward Sisters on the staff of St John's.

'You should be on Outpatients under Moaning Minnie. She never shouts at anybody; just whines everything. It makes one want to bash her with the nearest crutch. I say, are you all right?'

'I twisted myself turning a heavyweight. What's here, West?' She was patting her abdomen thoughtfully.

'That should be your uterus. I say, Kingston, what a round little tummy you're getting!'

'Oh, shut up! You sound like Cunliffe, one-track-minded.'

'Well, I didn't mean anything. I'm sorry.'

May gritted her teeth suddenly. There was no doubt but that the pain was racking her again and that it was a terrible sort of pain which didn't stop until one cried out.

'Shall I get Sister?' asked Margaret in real concern.

'No. Oh, no. I'll be all right. I have some codeine in my bag if you'll pass it. They're for any sort of pain, aren't they?'

When the pain had subsided she felt almost herself again, merely tired.

'I'll go to sleep,' she announced. 'The

142

others are on late duty, aren't they?'

'Yes. What about supper?'

'I'm not hungry. If Sister dining-room asks about me tell her I already told Sister Gibson my stomach is upset.'

May didn't sleep. Shortly after Nurse West had left the room she had more violence of pain and warm, sticky wetness surged from her body. There was a bell on the wall beside the door, but she found she had no strength to reach it. The violence went on for a long time and left her drained and drowsily sad that something which should have been so grand and fulfilling was so miserably ended.

Cunliffe and Henderson came banging into the room together after late supper at nine o'clock. Jean Cunliffe enjoyed her reputation of comedienne, but she was a nurse first and foremost.

'Oh lord, lord!' she cried out as she took in the scene. 'Her bed looks like a battlefield. Go and get Sister, Moira, and run like the devil. This is haemorrhage with a capital H. Poor old Kingston looks gone to me. Tell Sister I can't get a pulse.'

*   *   *

'Call Path,' said Mark tersely. 'We've got another bleeder here. It looks like she's

143

miscarried.'

'She's one of the nurses,' Sheila said from the phone. 'I saw her only this morning, having a cry. It appears she had something to cry about.'

Mark said, 'Poor little beggar! She's far gone. Nurse, the trolley, please. I'll cut down and hope for the best. Would you find the bleeder and plug it up, Doctor?'

They both worked fast. The pathologist on duty arrived like a milkman with several bottles of group 'O' blood in a metal holder.

'Right,' said Mark, 'let's get started.'

'I think it's too late,' said Sheila, letting the limp wrist go and holding the back of her hand against the parted, pallid lips.

'We'll try a spot of massage,' said Mark. 'She may have gone into shock. Who is the kid, anyway?'

May was still in her crumpled uniform dress. Sheila took a pair of scissors out of the pocket and read the name tape.

'Kingston,' she announced, and felt in the pocket more deeply as Mark pounded into the chest. 'Hello, what's this? It's a wedding ring on a string. Do you think she could be married?'

'A fat lot of good that will do her now. I'm not having any luck here, only bruising the body, so I'll have to give up. She's gone,

Sheila. She's gone.'

'Yes, I know. We're not equipped to bring them back from wherever she is.'

Mark was dismantling the transfusion apparatus. 'You'd better phone the Home Sister to tell her it was no go.'

Sheila came back looking glum. 'Sister Callaghan is coming over, and Gibson, too. The girl worked on her ward. She's an only child and comes from the North.'

'What a mess it all is!' Mark ran his hands through his thick hair. 'You know we're not supposed to feel for our patients? We're supposed to think it's only a job and any job is done more efficiently if one remains detached and unemotional? Well, I may or may not be a good doctor, but I feel blooming emotional about things like this. This morning she was combing her pretty brown hair and donning one of those ridiculous butterfly caps probationers wear, and tonight she's lying there as dead as a doornail and she'll be something pushed away on the mortuary trolley, under a sheet, and kept on ice until morning for the coroner to see. Poor, lonely, silly little kid!'

'I'll make some coffee,' Sheila offered.

'You're always making coffee,' he snapped. 'Is it your placebo, or something?'

She snapped back, 'It's something to do. I

don't like being no use, either. I hate them to die.'

He said, 'Sorry. Yes, I would like some coffee. My trouble is I'm not getting any sleep.'

'Why not?'

'I had a date with Martha to help her buy her new car.'

'And did she?'

'Yes. It's a Porsche. A beautiful thing.'

'So now you have the MG?'

'No,' he shrugged, looking away. 'She decided to hang on to it for the time being. I shall keep looking around.'

'My cousin Bob—he's a dentist—has a TR7 he wants to sell. I know it's a good car because dentists are far better off than we are, and his only reason for selling is that he's now married and they're expecting a baby. He feels he needs a saloon type so that there's room for the carry-cot. They motor a lot because his parents live in Torquay and hers are up in Suffolk. Naturally the baby will be shown off to all the grandparents.'

'Is it still for sale?'

'It was before I came on night duty. He rang me up asking if I could put an advert in the hospital house-mag for him. So far I haven't done it.'

'Could you tell him I'm interested? Could I

see it tomorrow?'

'What about all this sleep you're missing?'

'Well, some things are worth missing one's sleep for. Where does Bob practise?'

'In North London. Look'—she sounded embarrassed—'I don't want to push in, but I have a car, such as it is, and I could take you to see Bob tomorrow. I'll give him a ring in the morning and let you know if it's still available. Will that be all right?'

His mouth twisted. 'If you can stand my company I'm not going to look a gift filly in the mouth. And'—he added meaningly—'I got the message yesterday, and on my oath there'll be no messing about. You can feel quite safe even in the middle of the Sahara.'

'We don't cross the Sahara to get to Bob's,' she smiled. She wanted to say that the 'messing about' wasn't really so objectionable as she was now quite, quite free to play her part in it. But Mark had hinted last night that it was only a pleasurable game with him when they kissed, whereas she had taken it seriously, and too much of it, without a natural conclusion, would quickly break her heart. She was trying to make up her mind to accepting her career as her whole life. If one never looked for distraction one could no doubt do very well, maybe go abroad and work for a bit or go up and down the country

147

acting as *locum tenens* to doctors who needed a holiday or were ill. In a way it was all very exciting; secondarily exciting; for the most wonderful thing in the world was to be in love and for things to end with a happy-ever-after, whatever that involved.

★   ★   ★

Home Sister was upset when the sheet was raised and she recognised one of her flock.

'She miscarried, you say?' she almost wept. 'Oh, dear! She didn't tell anybody about it, and we could have helped her. It's not the end of the world, poor lamb! And what's this about a wedding ring? Now we have to follow it all up at Somerset House. They'll have a record of any wedding no matter how quiet the little minx kept it. I suppose this means a young husband somewhere in for a shock. Oh, me! Poor little Nurse! So young and—all over. I shan't sleep a wink this night.'

Fortunately both doctors were soon so busy they couldn't fret over the dead girl any longer, and while one was splinting up a suspected greenstick fracture for the night, and the other was giving an emetic to a child who had swallowed a dozen orange-flavoured aspirin tablets, the mortuary attendants appeared and took her away.

CHAPTER NINE

Miss Hattie's cottage was old and low-eaved, so low, in fact, that from the gate it looked like a small, fat man in a hat which was pulled down too far over his eyes. Its walls were of sturdy brick and flint, and the roof, which had once been thatched, was now of blue-speckled tiles. It sat in its colourful garden with the firm assurance of one who has been there a long time and seen a lot, and will still be there to watch a succession of owners go their way into eternity. It was a house with a look of permanence about it, a house meant to stand alone in a winding country lane; it was built to withstand the rigours of winter and the summer sun; it was full of odd corners and an awkward staircase revealed bedrooms which led off in surprising places, either one step up or two down. It contained twenty-five doors and admitted to eight different levels; it was hard work, expensive to run, old-fashioned, ugly and wholly delightful.

Next to the old house rose the monstrosity. This was an affair of two white cubes, one sitting to one side of the larger cube, which was the ground floor of the ultra-modern, open-plan house. Though it was supposed to have been conceived by an architect, Miss Hattie couldn't believe anyone could live with such a thing on his conscience. It fitted into the country scene as happily as a coster-monger's barrow and had about as much character as a railway arch. How impertinently its wide windows stared at Miss Hattie's gables! No wonder it housed a boy who stared also; who just stared and stared and stared at both Miss Hattie and Goliath, her marmalade cat.

The boy's father was in the American Air Force, and the family was awful, in Miss Hattie's opinion, with loud nasal voices, a car as ostentatious as a caravan and a freedom of manner which she cared to regard as plain rude and thoughtless.

Miss Hattie thought that of all the crosses she had to bear, her American neighbours were the heaviest cross of all. She had been waging a bitter feud with them for months before they even became aware of it. She finally made her point when she returned the boy's ball, before he had a chance to retrieve it himself, which he did often and unquestioningly through a convenient gap in the hedge. She said, 'Little boy, you are not to come through there again, do you hear? I am having the hedge stopped up. If you throw your ball over I shall keep it.'

The boy stared as usual for a moment, then he turned and called clearly towards the cube house.

'Mom! The old lady does talk, though she talks kinda funny. I don't think she takes a shine to me.'

Really! Little heathen! thought Miss Hattie. Old lady, indeed! She regarded herself critically in the hall mirror after that. Despite the shadows she acknowledged the fact that, dressed as she was, for gardening, in Father's hob-nailed boots, an old brat and leghorn straw hat, her hair descending in grey wisps wherever it had broken free of restricting pins, she made a very good picture of the Witch of Endor and must look positively archaic to a small boy.

Shortly afterwards she met the boy's father in the post-office. She tried to ignore him, but Americans are difficult people to ignore when they want to be noticed, and especially when they are one's neighbours.

'Ma'am,' he said, quite politely, 'ma'am, I'm sorry if the boy got in your hair. You see, ma'am, back home we don't put hedges between the yards. I guess he didn't understand.'

'That is quite all right,' Miss Hattie said coldly, 'so long as he knows now. When in Rome—you know? Here we *do* have hedges.'

151

The next horror was the dog they gave the boy. This dog was neither fish nor fowl, doggily speaking. Its antecedents might have been anything from mastiffs to hounds. It was large, hairy, playful, noisy, aggressive and happy. One of the creature's most distinguished moments was when it saw Goliath tiptoeing along the branch of a chestnut overhanging the hedge. It became so excited it threw a fit. Miss Hattie heard her male neighbour saying they would have to call the vet.

The next day 'Pooch', as they called the thing, was as right as rain again and lolloping all over the 'yard' in pursuit of the boy. It was Bedlam.

Goliath took to sulking and went off his favourite fish. Miss Hattie felt the dog was to blame. It was making poor Goliath's life a misery. He had only to show himself for the other creature to go mad, barking shrilly and hurling itself at the newly planted shoots of privet blocking the erstwhile gap. It would only be a matter of time before it could leap the hedge and tear poor Goliath limb from limb.

Before such a crisis could be reached, however, Miss Hattie penned a cold, polite little note requesting that her neighbours keep their dog under stricter control as her pet was of a nervous disposition.

They didn't reply in a like manner. Of course one doesn't expect foreigners to know what is what. The man waylaid her again as she was returning from the village and said, 'Gee, ma'am, we're sorry the pooch has been a bother. I guess we'll have to quieten him down a little.'

'I'm glad you think so.' She nodded and went on her way.

She found it difficult to feel pleased when she next saw the dog tied securely to a stake. It was hopelessly entangled in a length of line and howled pitifully. Its howl was louder than its bark. It wasn't the sort of dog which can look dignified when captive.

She deliberately hardened the heart which had no right to feel sentimental about what was only right. There was Goliath to consider. He rallied as he tucked into a slice of lamb's liver, dutifully drank his saucer of cream and stalked off to clean his whiskers.

She saw no more of him until late afternoon when she went out to hoe the large rose-bed. The dog next door was barking excitedly and, looking up, she observed Goliath trespassing in the neighbouring garden, positively wearing the jeering smile of a cat full of liver and cream with time—and mischief—on his paws and knowing his enemy is just out of reach.

'Goliath!' called Miss Hattie. 'Come back here, now! Do you hear?'

Goliath merely winked amber eyes and defied her. The dog was now tied up like a ball of knitting and fell over as fast as he stood up.

When Goliath deigned to return he received the first and only spanking of his life at the hands of his beloved. In his surprise and indignation he ran straight up to the top of the horse-chestnut and glowered down at her.

He refused to come down when it was time for 'beddie-byes'. Miss Hattie minced his fish, cooed and called. He mewed, but stayed where he was. By midnight Miss Hattie was in tortures. Goliath never had spent a night out of doors in his life. She heard his mewing and fancied he was trapped. Dressing in a warm flannel gown, she took a torch and went out into the garden, calling and clicking her tongue encouragingly. Despite the lateness of the hour her neighbours arrived home, probably from some party, happily and noisily.

'Just as well I wasn't asleep,' growled Miss Hattie, and called for Goliath softly and persistently to come and spend the night in his own comfortable basket.

'Excuse me, ma'am. Is anything wrong?'

The man in his uniform was actually in *her*

garden and standing behind her. She bit back the rebuke on her lips, however. Young men could climb, and Goliath had to be rescued by somebody.

'My cat is up in the tree,' she explained, and never knew why she added a lie. 'Your dog frightened him and he won't come down.'

'Gee, I'm sorry.'

In the dark she had the grace to blush. All this young man had ever said to her was 'I'm sorry.' Could it be that she, sometimes, was in the wrong?

'You don't think he'll be all right till morning? It is a bit late.'

'I think he might catch pneumonia again. He had it once, very badly, which is why I coddle him a little.'

'Well, we must get him then, ma'am, for sure. Have you a ladder?'

'Father's ladder. Still in the garage. This is very kind of you.'

'Only neighbourly, ma'am. I was brought up to be neighbourly.'

Again Miss Hattie blushed.

The ladder was brought and pushed up into the foliage of the burgeoning chestnut. The moon was now sailing brightly in the heavens and the torch made an artificial yellow circle of inadequate light. There was a rustling among the leaves then the torch showed

155

high up.

'I see him. Coochy, cooochy, here, boy!'

Goliath came silently and easily down the tree, his trickery exposed for what it was, and rubbed himself against Miss Hattie's legs.

'Thank you!' she called. 'He has come down.'

There was the rustling again and then the sight of a well-shod foot seeking the top rung of the ladder.

In the torchlight she saw it happen. Father's ladder was, of course, very old. She saw the rung snap cleanly in half and ladder and man arrived with a crash on the lawn together.

Miss Hattie fluttered. The torch had shot off and only in the unreal green moonlight did she notice the young man was in no hurry to stand up. Once again he apologised.

'I'm sorry, ma'am, to be such a nuisance, but I've bust something. Would you call my wife?'

*　　*　　*

It was only in dire emergency that a radiographer was called out at night. Most fractures could be splinted up until morning, but when Mark Leighton had examined the crew-cut young American pilot, had stuck pins in his nether limbs without raising one whimper of complaint, he frowned meaningfully at his colleague and signalled her outside the cubicle.

'I want X-rays taken, disturbing the patient as little as possible, and the senior orthopod in the hospital, and I want them stat. This is one that won't wait until morning.'

Soon the department was athrong with strangers who arrived with eyes heavy from sleep but were soon alerted by the nature of the emergency. With Captain Jacobson in expert hands the night staff assumed a minor role and were given the job of telling Mrs Jacobson the bad news. She was accompanied by a funny old woman with skimpy grey hair in pigtails and wearing an old flannel dressing-gown.

'Mrs. Jacobson . . . ?' Mark began, and looked at the older woman. 'Is this your mother?'

'No, no, I'm a neighbour,' said Miss Hattie. It was the first time she had ever called herself that or wanted to be one. She put her plump arms round the younger woman's shoulders as though anticipating the blow that was to fall.

'Your husband has fractured his spine,' Mark went on, 'and the right hip is cracked. Could you tell me what happened, exactly?'

Mrs Jacobson reeled and Sheila caught her,

pulled her head down, and then gave her a dose of sal volatile.

'Is Hal gonna die?' the woman asked quietly.

'No. He's going to be all right in time. It may be a long time.'

'Hal won't be able to fly again?'

Mark gave his answer frankly. 'Not as a pilot—no.'

'Then he's as good as dead. You hear me?' her voice crescendoed into a screech. 'Kill him! You hear me? Kill him! Flying's his life.'

Again an imperceptible nod from Mark to his colleague which she interpreted as, 'Sedate her, quickly.'

When Mrs Jacobson was quiet, weeping softly to herself, Mark turned once more to the neighbour.

'Madam, can you tell me what happened?'

'Yes, I can.' Miss Hattie told the story as it had happened. Mark couldn't quite believe it.

'You mean'—he indicated the treatment-room behind them and the figures flitting within, visible through the frosted glass—'all this was for a wretched cat?'

Miss Hattie bridled.

'Young man, Goliath may be a wretched cat to you, but to me he is my devoted companion of the past fourteen years.'

Mark snorted, and Sheila looked anxious.

158

Her colleague's patience was easily tried, she knew.

'Would everybody like a cup of tea?' she asked placatingly.

'Oh, my God!' Mrs Jacobson said dully, through the sedation. 'The babysitter's still there. I gotta go home.'

'No, no,' said Miss Hattie. 'You must stay here near your husband, my dear. Let me go and look after things. You are not to worry. I'm really very handy.'

She gave an appealing glance up at Mark which said, 'Look, I'm doing what I can—being a good neighbour.'

But Mark was watching the operation of a crippled flier being strapped to a special spinal bed. He was laughing and joking.

'Hey, what gives? I got no pain. What've I busted? You fellers gotta be kidding.'

Sheila said when all was quiet again and the department back to normal, 'This is being what I call a bad night; bad cases. I hope they've finished.'

'This is also a bad time of a bad night,' he added. 'Three-thirty, and I feel a deep depression coming on.'

'How about lying down for an hour?'

'No. As long as you're upright I, too, shall stay vertical.'

'I'm sorry I can't think of anything to
159

relieve a deep depression.'

'I can,' he said meaningfully, 'but I'll be a man and overcome it.'

★   ★   ★

Things always seem better in daylight. Sheila had arranged to meet Mark in the dining-room for breakfast.

'I phoned Bob and his TR is still available. I suggest we meet at the gates about four o'clock. That should give us seven hours' sleep comfortably.'

'Right-ho. If this comes off I shall insist on regarding you as my guardian angel. I know there was some some reason for us meeting up again! Have the bacon and sausages. This kipper would make a good sole if anybody has a hole in their shoe. I was going to complete my thesis this week, but with one thing and another—'

'Could I read it—your thesis?'

'Mm—yes, if you want to. I'll get it back from Martha. She has it at the moment.'

He became very thoughtful as he remembered Martha.

CHAPTER TEN

Word spread through the student ranks from those who had volunteered for night duty and now looked jaded and crumpled, unshaven and grey-cheeked.

'One of the nurses died during examination. She miscarried.'

'Fast little beggar! She's paid the price of her sin. Who can lend me half a dollar for my breakfast?'

Bernard Hull was one of the last to hear. His stomach cramped and he vomited.

'Hi! You'll never make a doc if you faint when you hear about death. They say blood was all over everything. She never had a chance.'

'Who—who was she?'

'How do I know? They're legion in there. She was a brunette. But they all die if they haemorrhage sufficiently, dark and fair, fat and thin.'

Bernard knew it was May. His first feelings after the nausea were of relief. It was all over. There was nothing left to alienate his Jewish parents, her Chapel-happy folk. He did wonder how it had happened and whether she had done something she shouldn't. He found he couldn't forget about it, though, and eventually went to see an older student who occasionally acted as his unpaid mentor.

'Silverman, can I speak with you for a minute?'

'A minute I can spare. Then I have a lecture. Well?'

'This may sound a stupid thing to ask, but just supposing you were secretly married and you were wanting to keep it a secret. Could anybody find out?'

'Is this a hypothetical question, or do we know somebody in this predicament?'

'Well, no. Yes, actually, I do. I promised not to split.'

'Then I would say that providing his wife's in the secret they shouldn't have any difficulty keeping it, if that's their intention. They wouldn't have to do anything stupid like her getting pregnant, of course.'

'Well, actually, that did happen. It complicated things rather.'

'I should say it did! Babies have a habit of growing until they're born. Obviously your friend hasn't a hope of keeping his secret much longer. I presume he's one of us? Well, my advice is for him to tell all to the Dean and see what comes of it.'

'He won't be kicked out?'

'I doubt it. He'll be called every sort of fool,

of course, but I suppose even the Dean has been young and stupid in his time. But the main problem is the wife and the child she's bearing. She must be his constant and only concern.'

'Yes, Silverman, but actually she miscarried and died.'

'You mean the girl last night?'

'Yes. Oh, I'm giving so much away and I promised. My friend is wondering now if he need say anything, if there's any way they'll find him out. The girl never told anyone, not even her parents. It wasn't a very suitable match, you see. If he keeps quiet...'

David Silverman's face shrunk until every feature was narrowed and super-critical. He appeared to veer away from the other as from a bad smell.

'Your minute's more than up,' he announced, 'and tell your friend, from me, that I think he stinks.'

Bernard looked after him and wanted to crawl under a stone.

*   *   *

Bernie Hull looked up at the craggy face of the Dean, the disciplinary officer of the Medical School, and felt he was for it. He rather hoped he was, having need to clothe himself in

163

sackcloth and ashes. The Dean was merely kind, however.

'Well, I suppose you've suffered enough, boy, without me calling you every kind of a fool. If it had to be you should have told us. We're not inhuman monsters. Of course we discourage students from marrying, but if they do it then it's better out. Your wife lay there and bled to death alone. She should have been in your arms. Don't you feel that?'

'Oh, sir, it hasn't really sunk in yet. May was—was so alive the last time I saw her.'

'And carrying your child, boy. Two lives have been sacrificed by this pact of secrecy. Do you understand?' The phone on the Dean's desk rang. 'Come on! We've got to get over there. Your parents-in-law have arrived.'

'My—*what*?'

'Your wife's parents.'

Bernie stared dumbly at the ordinary-looking couple who were devoured partly by grief and shock, but mostly hostility.

'We're upset. May should have told us,' the woman said fretfully. 'Not knowing was bad.'

'Hole and corner affair,' grumbled Mr Kingston. 'What was there to hide, eh?'

'We were in love,' said Bernie stupidly. 'In love.' There was no reaction from May's parents. He knew that they thought love was vaguely obscene and nice people didn't speak of it.

'What's done is done, I suppose.' Mrs Kingston's voice implied that all had ended as well as could be expected. 'We've just come to get her, to take her home.'

Bernie felt the need to make one gesture. May had made them all—suffered the pain, shed her blood, died alone, kept their secret.

'I don't think you understand,' he now pronounced in the chill gloom of the hospital mortuary. 'May was my wife. I have a marriage certificate—everything. I'm legally of age and answerable to nobody and I shall take care of her, now. You're not taking her anywhere. I—I'm sorry.'

There were arguments, long and bitter and acrimonious. The Dean opined that a husband had his unassailable rights. Bernie, who wondered how he was going to pay the funeral expenses, still didn't budge. It was later that he cried, and then because the coffin looked so small. May was only five foot two and he had often teased her about her lack of inches. On his wreath of white roses, he wrote 'Better to have loved and lost...' Her parents didn't come to the funeral and his weren't invited. For a couple of days Bernard Hull wished he was dead, and then he recovered and worked towards becoming the best student of his year.

'You know,' said Mark, 'that wasn't bad driving, for a woman.'

Sheila grimaced at his purely masculine compliment which was always an insult.

'Statistics show we have very few fatal accidents,' she told him, 'and neither have we a desire to beat everything else on the road.'

'This,' observed Mark, looking round the interior of the Mini, which cramped his long legs, 'couldn't beat a carpet. But'—he smiled expansively—'it may get us to London before lighting-up time, if we're lucky.'

'Oh, you're so superior,' said she, 'on your way to buy your sports model. My old Emily has given me good service and I'm very fond of her.'

'You know,' he said suddenly, 'I don't know what to talk about with you, since a certain subject is taboo.'

'We have our work in common,' she said quickly. 'Why not talk about that? Did you bring your thesis?'

'Yes. I got it back off Martha just before I came out.'

'This is all scribbled out and corrected,' said Sheila as they stopped at traffic lights and she looked within the large envelope he had placed in the glove compartment.

'I know. One has lots of second thoughts about things. See if you can make sense of it, because the idea of writing it all out afresh, in longhand, before it goes to the typist appals me.'

'I have a typewriter in my room,' Sheila volunteered. 'I can type.' There followed a silence heavy with expectancy. 'Would you like me to do it?' she asked.

'Would you?'

'Certainly. In our job we should help each other out.'

'You know,' he grinned, 'I'm just finding out you're a very nice girl. Being in love does rather cloud one's judgment, and up there among the stars one's view is pathetically distorted. Would you prefer to have somebody worship you as a goddess or be thought a nice girl?'

'To be frank I would prefer my husband to worship and my friends to like me. Is that greedy?'

'No. Count me among your most admiring friends in that case.'

They were now threading through the London traffic of early evening, so he left her to concentrate on her driving and remembered his earlier seeking-out of Martha with a hard look in his eyes. She had been on the men's ward.

'Yes, Mr Leighton, what are you doing here?' she had demanded.

'Actually I would like my thesis, Martha. I—'

'Here on the ward I'm Miss Haley to my houseman, if you don't mind.'

'Oh. Sorry. Look, Martha, I mean Miss Haley, do we have to be like this? I mean we're both adults, and—'

'Mr Leighton, I now very much doubt your statement. I seem to remember you were a scared rabbit who couldn't get out of my flat quickly enough. But that is past history and doesn't concern me any longer. What does concern me is that Sir William is now having doubts about keeping you on his firm. Young Doane is shaping up very well and, frankly, we feel he ought to be encouraged. You haven't been missed during your absence.'

Anger had seethed through Mark. She had Sir William in her elegant pocket, of course, and was letting him know he was, from this moment, out on his ear as far as she was concerned.

'Has Doane been subjected yet to the strip-tease treatment?' he asked, feeling stung.

Her hand struck out and lashed him, leaving a scarlet stain across his cheek. She pushed the large envelope containing his thesis at him. 'Now get out!' she told him,

168

with all the fury of the proverbial woman scorned.

He calmed and tucked the envelope under his arm. What it contained was really the directive of his future, not this nymphomaniac with her lewd posturings.

Bob Devaney was pleased to see his cousin and her companion, and Mark soon fell in love with the Triumph.

'Take Sheila for a spin,' invited Bob. 'Really get the feel of it.'

'Now this,' said Mark, 'is a beaut. A man should have three things in this modern world; a good car, any sort of a boat and then a woman. She definitely comes third. The poor suckers who put her first rarely get the other two until they're too old and tied up to enjoy them.'

'Thank goodness I knew you before you were a cynic,' said Sheila. 'Now that you've almost got a car, are you thinking of buying a boat?'

'I have a small cabin-cruiser laid up at Marlow. I spend all my leave in her. She's a roof over my head *and* a boat.'

'So you don't really need a woman at all, do you? Even housekeeping on a small boat can't be beyond you.'

'Now who's the cynic? One can't make love to a boat.'

'But then, way down the list as she is, your other pleasures are obvious priorities.'

'It's nice to hear a woman admit it.'

'I didn't admit it. I—' She desisted, knowing she was being teased or taunted.

'Well, thanks for putting me on to this,' he said as they drew up again outside Bob's elegant house. 'The engine's clean, the brakes really bite and the upholstery's super. There's just a scratch or two on the passenger side to attend to, but I suppose any car in London is lucky to get away with scratches. I'll need to get a licence and an insurance cover-note before I can take it away.'

Bob, however, was so delighted at having made the sale that he promised to deliver it to St John's next morning, and this arrangement appeared to make Mark's day.

'I thought the MG was IT,' he said, 'but the powers that be knew better. Miss Haley had ground the gears a bit and there was a faulty door-catch.'

'Miss Haley?' queried Sheila. 'I thought she was Martha to you?'

'Hm,' he said, non-committally, then smiled happily. 'I'll go down to Marlow in my car when I've finished my night-stint and spend my thirty-six hours in the *Lady Verity*. That will be very nice. Having to rely on trains for transport is no use for thirty-six hours. This is going to make a big difference to me, I can tell you.'

'Well, couldn't you have borrowed Martha's MG any time? I know you could have borrowed this.'

'Thanks,' proudly, 'but I'm only a borrower when I have something with which I can pay back. I can't think of anything you could ask of me.'

'Oh, if only you knew!' she cried silently.

'Martha, too, has everything already. When I borrowed the MG it was with a view to purchasing. But I told you, that deal fell through.'

'I wonder why? I've seen a dark blue Porsche in the parking area.'

'Maybe she got a better offer. Anyhow, no matter. I'm well content with my bargain. By the way'—he thought he had better anticipate any curiosity she might have about his future activities—'I may be leaving Sir William's firm.'

'Oh? I thought it was all settled and that it was only a matter of time before you became one of his registrars. You really can't afford to cock a snook at consultants of Sir William's calibre.'

'I'm actually thinking of emigrating.' This was the first time he had thought of any such thing, but the idea immediately appealed to him.

'Oh, you can't!' was torn from her.

'Why ever not? I have no ties here. Mother is very independent.'

'I suppose there's no reason really.'

'Exactly. I want to get on and I find there's still something remarkably like nepotism goes on here. If you're nobody and have no influential friends you don't get anywhere.'

'But you have Sir William,' she assured him. 'Who more influential than he?'

He felt there could be no half-truths between them. She demanded and expected absolute honesty of him as he did of her.

'I've discovered,' he said, 'that Martha Haley has been speaking up for me to Sir William. *She* has really been my sponsor, and I don't want my future to depend on the whim of a woman.'

'I can understand that,' she agreed.

'Women can be terribly unscrupulous,' he had to add, 'you can't trust them like men.'

'You're generalising, as usual. Some women are scrupulous and some are not. Even some men are less than archangels.'

'You are very argumentative nowadays, Sheila. I'm glad I found you out.'

'*You* found *me* out?'

'Watch where you're going. You're carrying precious cargo; the new owner of a Triumph

Spitfire Mark Seven, no less.'

She crumpled up into laughter, then sobered again.

'Try your luck in England before you decide to emigrate,' she urged.

'Well, it really all depends on the contents of that packet, doesn't it? When it's Mark Meredith Leighton, MD, I'll be dealing from strength.'

'I never knew about the Meredith bit before.'

'Didn't you? Actually I keep it dark. Meredith was my mother's maiden name.' The hospital hove into view. 'Well, thanks for the trip, Sheila. You've been delightful company, as ever. I hope Bruce realises he's getting a treasure.'

She couldn't tell him for the life of her that Bruce was now in the past. She feared the change in Mark if he fancied she might have cleared the way to hunt anew. It was one thing to play at being in love, but when one was taken seriously then one might wish to step back over the line of demarcation and think again.

It was still light when they scrambled out of the car at nine o'clock, and they were observed, from her room, by Martha Haley. She saw the little car and with amazement and resentment watched Mark extricate himself, followed by a pretty, fair girl she had seen around.

'So that must be his wonderful Sheila!' she almost spat. 'That's what he prefers to me. Oh, how can I hurt him more?' she demanded, pacing like a caged lioness. 'I have never been so humiliated before in all my life. I could have given him everything. *Everything*. But now I only want to take away and deprive him of what he has. I won't let him get away with what he did to me. He'll remember the name of Martha Haley long after he's forgotten about Sheila!'

*   *   *

'We've got a rough hour ahead,' Mark announced. 'This one's a lulu. The silly girl has perforated her appendix with a strong purgative and she's jibbing at the idea of immediate operation. As she's of age, in years at least, we have to get her signature on the consent form and get on with it. You might have a go at her and hurry.'

Sheila entered the cubicle and closed the curtains behind her. What did Mark mean by 'of age, in years at least'? The girl looked intelligent and was very pretty, her eyes burning in fever.

'Hello!' Sheila greeted.

'How d'you do?' The girl paused and grimaced in pain. 'I want to—' Sheila put the vomit-bowl to her lips, turning her head to the side. The vomit was typically green and thick. She wiped the girl's face with a tissue and smiled reassuringly.

'The sooner we get you done the better, young lady. I have a consent-form I want you to sign.'

'No—no operation,' the girl gasped, turning her head from side to side. 'Give me antibiotics or something. I can't have an operation.'

'Is your objection on religious grounds?'

'Good lord, no! My set isn't at all religious.'

'Then you're scared?'

'Of course. But that's not the reason. I can't possibly go to Deauville in the autumn with a scar on my tum. Nicole Messiter had one, and she couldn't wear a bikini. It was all drawn and tuckered.'

Now Sheila knew what Mark meant. This girl thought more of her appearance, apparently, than her life.

'I don't know who your friend's surgeon was, but I can assure you that at your age your skin is extremely elastic and the surgeon will use this elasticity, leaving you with a small scar which should fade almost completely in time.'

175

'Oh, God! I need it again.' The vomiting was torment. The girl looked at Sheila pleadingly. 'Can't you give me something for the pain?'

'There's no point, because the pain is going to increase considerably.'

'What's the alternative to operation?' Sheila decided to be brutal.

'This time tomorrow you'll be dead, Amanda. You won't be going to Deauville this or any year unless we operate quickly.'

'I knew you'd do it,' Mark said with a smile, taking the signed consent-form. 'It takes one woman to understand another.'

'I've promised her a beautiful scar,' Sheila said, 'so who's doing it?'

'I am, with your assistance.' She stared at him. 'There's a bit of a hoo-ha going on up in Surgical "A" unit, a colostomy case has collapsed and they're opening him up immediately in main theatres. We're to take over the emergency theatre and the RSO will come along later to see how we're doing. A couple of housemen are taking over here.'

A green-clad, turbaned nurse came to take Amanda for preparation, giving her her pre-med immediately.

'I've never actually assisted at a major operation,' said Sheila timidly. 'Couldn't we find somebody more experienced?'

176

'Of course I could, but you've got to learn something before you go into general practice. You can clamp, can't you, and swab? I'll be telling you what to do, in any case, so just keep alert and listen.'

The Sister in charge of the emergency theatre, looked somewhat disapprovingly at the unimportant hospital small fry she had been told to assist. She was an ex-theatre Sister, had even 'scrubbed' for a couple of years in the States, and when Mr Leighton objected to the gown in which she was enfolding him she thought it cheek.

'I can't operate in a shroud, Sister. Something shorter and sweeter, if you please.'

'I didn't think we were having a theatre fashion show at this time of night, sir . . .'

Mark regarded the older woman levelly.

'Some people find it impossible to garden in gloves, Sister, and others have eccentricities like fluffing up cushions and straightening pictures. My little oddity is hating to see drapery about my person; I begin to feel I'm in a tent. Now, may I have a short gown, please?'

'Certainly, sir.' Mark gave Sheila a meaningful glance as they continued to scrub.

'Don't grow like that,' he warned, 'full of your own self-importance.'

'I probably shall,' she said ruefully.

'I'm glad I won't be there to see it.'

Sheila felt weak for a moment as she saw the scalpel cut through the skin and the incision fill with red.

'Swab!' Mark almost snapped, and she rallied and told herself she was assisting at a major operation, a great privilege she might not have experienced for months but for Mark. He cut through a layer of subcutaneous fat and then divided the muscle carefully, exposing an artery and calling 'clamp that!' clearly.

They were through to the peritoneum in no time, strangely moist and foul, and there was more swabbing to be done, then Mark sought the appendix, inflamed and discharging from the abscess formed to one side. This soon reposed in a kidney dish and Mark tied off the pedicle, calling clearly for everything he wanted. Sister was looking at him respectfully now; no consultant-surgeon of her acquaintance could have been quicker or more thorough. As a nurse she admired efficiency, but this apparently was not only given to the experienced in years.

There was more swabbing to be done, and everything was certainly much sweeter, then the organs were dusted with penicillin powder as they were replaced and the business of counting swabs went on before the clamps were removed and arteries and veins rejoined.

'How is she?' Mark asked the anaesthetist.

'Oh, she hasn't looked back. She's fine.'

'Then come and do some final embroidery, Dr Devaney,' Mark invited.

'Oh, sir, I—' His eyes warned her not to let him down, to trust his judgment.

He told her where to pierce the skin and where to tie between stitches.

'Go on!' he encouraged. 'She can't feel anything—yet. Make it firmer than that.' She hesitated and he explained, 'At the moment the muscles are relaxed. They will tighten up. She's the greyhound type. That'—he announced at last—'is a scar of which anybody could be proud. Sister—?' he enquired.

'Very nice, Doctor,' said Sister, now completely won over. 'We'll attract you to the surgical side, I hope, after a show like that?'

Sheila was pleased, and Mark spoilt her pleasure a little.

'No,' he said quite blithely. 'She's getting married and going into general practice. This, Sister, is one that is getting away.'

'Oh, is that so?'

Sheila thought she had better at least hint.

'Nothing is absolutely firm yet,' she volunteered to the company as Mandy was wheeled off to the recovery room. 'If I thought I had the makings of a surgeon I might be tempted.'

'Don't you dare, Doctor,' Sister promptly shot her down. 'Getting married is still a woman's top-priority job. Anybody who tells you differently is not only frustrated but downright jealous. I thought my job was more important when I was twenty-five.'

'She doesn't need encouragement to go ahead, Sister,' observed Mark as his soiled gown was whisked off him and away. 'This is a very determined young woman.'

As they scrubbed again, Sheila asked, in some irritation, 'Did you have to tell everybody about me? I'm sure they weren't really interested.'

'I'm sorry. Did I make you self-conscious? I thought Sister gave you rattling good support.'

'She did. But it just so happens that things are not exactly as they were when you and I discussed them. I saw Bruce yesterday and—well, we're not engaged any more.' Her voice trembled into silence and he saw her lips quivering, her eyes lowered.

'I'm sorry,' he said, misunderstanding. 'These middle-aged codgers are often very set in their ways. You must have been feeling rotten and yet you haven't shown by a single sign. I can only repeat—I'm sorry.'

'Thank you.' She buried her face into a

towel. What had she expected? That Mark would say, 'Well, can I step back into your life?' Things didn't happen like that. Many men were wonderful lovers but baulked at the idea of being husbands. They had an ingrained idea that their masculine talents should be spread around.

'Back to the grind,' Mark stated. 'Although we've given a star performance we still have to get on with the humdrum jobs of a night cas stint. It's still only midnight. How time does drag! Is this our third or fourth night together?'

'The fourth. Two to go.'

'Well, I don't know whether to say good, all bad things come to an end or bad, all good things ditto.'

'You probably want to get this night stint over with, as I do, and continue with your serious job.'

'But what *is* my serious job? I suppose you have a nice comfortable ward waiting to receive you, your life ordered the next few months, but I've reached a sort of Rubicon. Anyhow, I don't want to bore you with my affairs.'

'I'm not bored. I'm not so wrapped up in myself that I can't listen to someone else.'

They reached Casualty and nodded to the two housemen who had been holding the fort.

'Anything much happen?' asked Mark, consulting the log.

'Not much, sir.' Sheila felt a glow of pride that housemen deferred to Mark as their senior. He was, of course, presenting his thesis and she was confident this would earn him his MD diploma. 'Small stuff. One foreign body removed from an eye, a suspected poisoning which wasn't, as it turned out, and a slight concussion which we've sent up to the ward just to be on the safe side.'

'Right, lads, get back to bed.'

'I have a feeling we'll be back, sir. It's one of those nights when everything happens.'

'The next thing which is happening is refreshment,' said Mark comfortably and assuredly. Nurse Collins, who had been reloading dressings, took the hint and could be heard rattling about in the kitchen.

'Why did you tell me to consider well before emigrating?' Mark asked, at length.

'Well,' she answered quickly, 'it's a big step and one should be very, very sure, I think.'

'Are you still going into general practice?'

'I—I don't know. I have nine months to complete here first, and then I may reach my Rubicon too.'

'It—it's quite over, is it? I mean no chance of second thoughts?'

'No chance. We're now out of touch.'

'It seems rotten. I mean you had your plans all set. He must be mad as well as blind, this Bruce.'

'What do you mean by that?' she asked in a thin high voice.

'Well—to let you go. Obviously he was getting the best of the bargain, a young, beautiful wife and a partner to boot.'

'It wasn't Bruce. *I* asked to be released. I felt terrible about it.'

'But why . . . ?'

'Must we discuss it?' she asked tersely. Why couldn't he see what was so plain to her, that she had only to be in his arms again to forget Bruce and any other man who had flitted through her life during those five years?

'I didn't mean to pry. Your business. But as it *has* happened, wouldn't *you* consider emigrating?'

'Good gracious!' she responded, and then the coffee arrived.

She wanted him to develop the theme, but instead he allowed the subject to drop, as though the exclamation had been a veto. He was silent as he sipped and she was painfully aware of his long, lean good looks and the total masculinity of his opinions.

'What'll you do with your thirty-six hours when you're relieved?' he finally asked.

'Probably sleep the clock round and then go

and see my mama,' she replied.

'Oh, I was going to say that if you're in the vicinity of Marlow, drop in.'

'Literally drop in the river?' she smiled.

'If you're getting frisky, Dr Devaney, it's time some more work was forthcoming, and that'—as the outside phone rang shrilly—'is probably it.'

'Always,' she thought, 'when my life is getting interesting a bell rings or somebody interrupts and it's extremely difficult to get back to the point again.'

Mark turned from the phone.

'Yon callow youth was right. Everything *is* happening tonight. We're going out to a fire. Staff Nurse!' Collins' round, plump brown face appeared round the lintel of the clinical-room. 'Get those fellows back, Staff, to cover. We'll be bringing in some burn cases, very likely. What degree I don't yet know. Lay on the necessary procedures. They'll have had the cold water treatment first.'

The stand-by ambulance team had been alerted and the vehicle was soon speeding to the scene of the fire, its ululating klaxon tearing the still of the night to shreds. There was little traffic and soon the acrid smell of burning hung heavily on the air. The fire had started in the kitchen of a small terraced house and had badly damaged the bedroom above

184

where four children had been sleeping. Now the fire was under control, and as the ambulance arrived the fourth child was being brought out by a fireman wearing breathing apparatus.

'I think this one's had it,' he announced as he removed the mask. 'It's never moved since I found it, poor little beggar!'

The other three children were lying some distance away, writhing and groaning while their father, helpless and smoke-blackened, tried to comfort them. The mother was in a sorry state, she was pleading like a mad thing, 'My baby! Where's my baby?'

Taking in the scene Mark said sharply, 'Right. Get the ambulance men to help you with the duckings of those three before loading them. I'm going to try mouth-to-mouth resuscitation on the baby.'

The scene was other-worldly to Sheila, who certainly was having plenty of excitement on her initiation to night duty. Helped by Bert, the ambulance number two, she poured cold water from a bucket on burnt hands, arms and one little buttock, before wrapping each child in sterile cotton topped by a blanket, and out of the corner of her eye saw Mark, in the light of a flare, forcing the breath from his own lungs into the collapsed lungs of a suffocated child. The baby piped suddenly and was sick,

185

and it was the sweetest sound in the world to Sheila, who wanted to cry because when a doctor restores life which has been lost it is a little miracle, and miracles are emotional things. The baby, as it happened, was the least badly burnt, and all four children were whipped away to receive the specialist care of the hospital burns unit.

'You did well,' Mark told his colleague as they changed soiled duty coats for clean ones.

'Thank you. I noticed you didn't do so badly, either.'

Staff Nurse Collins beheld them and said, 'OK. Don't say it. You want refreshment. Thank goodness Lewis is back tomorrow night and then she can carry the department on her own. But let me tell you, she has all the luck. Tomorrow night Matron will find she has another nurse to spare and Lewis will be laughing, as usual.'

Mark smiled at Sheila. 'Poor old Collins! She has a permanent sense of injury about something or other.'

'She told me these are the last two weeks of her period of night duty. I suppose she's jaded by now. To come from a land of eternal sunshine to spend three months regarding English nights!'

It was quiet and the dead hours of early morning were no longer quite so grim. Sheila thought, 'Just to be with Mark gives me a kind of peace inside.'

She jumped when he spoke. She had thought he was dozing, for his eyes were closed.

'Sheila, forgive me, but my thoughts have been jumping around like fleas for some time. I know you're a kind person and would want me to feel settled in my mind with all that lies ahead career-wise . . .'

'Of course, Mark. How can I settle your mind?'

'By being very honest with me and not hedging when I ask what you may consider an impertinent question' . . . Her eyes were watchful, but she kept them unwaveringly on his. . . 'When you broke your engagement was it because your feelings for Bruce had suddenly changed?'

'No,' she told him frankly, her heart racing in her chest.

'Oh.' He looked deflated. 'Thanks for telling me, anyway.'

'Why did you ask?' She couldn't allow the subject to drop again.

'Obviously because I wanted to know.'

'Why?'

'I had my reasons.'

'I know you had your reasons. Please be equally frank with me, Mark.'

He regarded her. His dark eyes were somehow pained as though they had gazed at the sun too long. He closed them again and spoke.

'It occurred to me, big-head that I am, that certain events we recently shared had changed your feelings towards Bruce, no matter how much against your will or how little they were inclined back towards me. That's all.'

'Oh.' Still her heart was knocking against her ribs. She decided that if a bell rang at that moment, or an interruption occurred, it would stop and she would die at Mark's feet. 'Well, my feelings didn't change.'

'So you said.'

'I decided they weren't the right feelings for marriage. They were of deep affection and respect only.'

His eyes shot open and there was a glow about them which burnt into hers.

'And had I anything to do with this?'

'Oh lord, yes!'

He jumped up and the too-small chair crashed to the floor behind him.

'Sheila?' he besought her.

'Mark, we're on duty,' she reminded him. She would be fit for nothing if he took her in his arms at that moment.

'I know. I know. I'm saying nothing at this time because I'm in no position to. But now I

188

feel I have every incentive. Sheila, you remember five years ago . . . ?'

'Yes, Mark?'

'I wrote a letter telling you that there just had to be an answer for us. It couldn't end like that in bitterness and frustration. I would wait, I said, and seek you out again when we had had time to think and miss each other. I was already missing you terribly. I wondered why you didn't answer, of course, but I still determined to have things out with you. Then when I went down with polio I decided I wouldn't be much good for any woman. They fumigated my clothes—the old tweed jacket I always wore among them—and they found an unposted letter in the lining bearing an outdated stamp. They asked did I still want it and I said no, it didn't matter.'

Sheila's eyes were wet.

'Trust you,' she said. 'What a difference getting that letter would have meant to me!'

'Anyway,' he said happily, 'here we are, despite all our efforts to the contrary.'

'Yes,' she agreed, 'here we are. I'm so glad, Mark.'

'I think you'd better come, Doctors,' said Nurse Collins. 'The night isn't over yet.'

Two of the student volunteers, in the middle of refilling depleted drums of dressings for sterilisation, were standing over the third student who was lying prone on the rubberised flooring.

'His pulse is a bit quick, sir,' said one youth, 'he just said he felt queer and fell down.'

Mark made a quick, expert examination, borrowing Sheila's ophthalmoscope to examine the collapsed man's pupils.

'Do you lads ever take drugs?' he asked casually.

'Oh, sir!'

'*Do you?*'

'Well, I have taken benzedrine occasionally when I've had to study late, sir.'

'Where do you get it?'

'One can apply to the RMO, sir.'

'I know one can apply. But does he give it to you?'

'Not very often, sir. He doesn't like us to start on stimulants before we have to.'

'Help me get this lad up on to a bed.' A little later Mark said, 'I'm going through his pockets. I want you all to be witnesses.'

The only things which interested Mark in an assortment of pens, knives, a brand-new stethoscope and oddments of small change were two small phials. One contained tablets of dexedrine, a stimulant which is a development of benzedrine, and the other, two-grain tablets of phenobarbitone.

'They're somewhat similar,' pronounced Mark, confiscating the phials, 'and I think he took the barbiturate by mistake. Enforced stimulation and equally enforced sedation, gentlemen, are wearing on the head when used indiscriminately. I don't mind my students going to sleep in corners at odd times, but I won't have them pepped up to the eyeballs, either. You can spread that through the ranks. I have to report this to the RMO in the morning, I'm sorry to say. What's the lad's name?'

'MacIntyre, sir, but please don't. He might be kicked out.'

Sheila also looked anxiously up at Mark.

'I can't keep quiet about a thing like this,' he said harshly. 'I have to write up a log, as you know. What year is he?'

'Third, sir. He's one of our best students.'

'Silly young fool, then. He'll probably be let off with a caution. Now get him on a trolley and push him off to bed. I can't stand the sight of him any longer.' He paced about like a tiger for a while after the students had gone. 'How can I suppress a thing like that?' he asked Sheila.

'Say he fainted?' she suggested.

He was all doctor as he regarded her, pityingly and faintly hostile.

'You know he didn't faint, so did those two.

Am I to put lies in the log now? I'm surprised at you. If we skate over this he'll hooch himself up again periodically until one day, maybe, he falls down—kaput! All over. I shall report the incident to the RMO as is right and proper, and if he passes the info on to the Dean of the Medical School, that's his business. Now I hope that's settled and there's to be no more argument or pleadings?'

'Of course you're right, Mark,' Sheila said humbly. 'I suppose I'm nearer the student level than you are and I can feel their panic, but if we're slipshod in our profession, mankind might as well give up.'

'Yes. You learn to think like that in future, young woman. There are no indeterminate stages between wrong and right as there are between black and white.'

She had a sudden notion.

'Why don't you apply for a teaching post in the School, Mark? I think the students would really look up to someone like you.'

'A tutor? Me? I can't see myself, somehow, and the young male, *en masse*, is a bit heavy going.'

'There are thirty per cent or more women every year, nowadays, join the school.'

'Now that *is* an inducement,' he laughed. 'I can only see one woman at a time and you'll do, Sheila. Keep some time next week free, I may want to propose.'

'Why next week?' she wanted to know, with a pout.

'Because I have things to do till then. I don't want anything to go wrong a second time.'

CHAPTER ELEVEN

Sheila was breakfasting leisurely when a young house physician with whom she had worked previously joined her at her table.

'Aren't you on night cas?' he asked.

'Yes.'

'Well, what's this about selling your drugs?'

'Whatever do you mean?'

'There's a real old stink going on about it. You do know that periodically there's a drug racket and how touchy the Governors are about such things? Apparently one of the students has been hauled up for being high on duty . . .'

'Actually he was low,' Sheila corrected. 'Very low. He had taken a barbiturate by mistake. I was there.'

'Well, your colleague had sold him drugs from stock. He said so. There's one hell of a hoo-hah going on.'

Sheila knew enough about most hospital gossip to realise that it was always rooted in fact. She fled in search of Mark and met him coming, thunder-browed, from the RMO's private office.

'They're saying—' she greeted him. 'Is it true?'

'That I sell hospital drugs to students? Do you believe that?'

'No, I don't believe that at all. I meant is it true that's what young MacIntyre said? The nerve of him!'

'He not only said it but practically swore an affidavit. I suppose his mates had warned him he was due for a showdown and he was all ready with the tar-brush and his lies. Not only he was going to suffer; he had made up his tiny mind. The RMO only narrowly believed me, I could see, so expert was his lordship at passing the buck. After all, the tablets had come from somewhere. They're not sold by the quarter like dolly-mixtures. Then, just when we were getting civilised again, there's a shriek from the regular CO that he's twenty-five phenobarbs down and eighteen tablets of dexedrine and can the night staff account for same. This MacIntyre bloke looks me straight between the eyes and says, "Now do you remember, sir? That's what you allowed me, and I gave you a ten-pound note." I just didn't know what to say, so I blew my top for five minutes. I'm now going to bed.'

'Mark, please listen!' she ran to keep up with him. 'I was with you all night. I can vouch for you.'

'And can you explain how the drug cupboard was raided? I had the keys except when they were handed over to the relief staff. If there's an official enquiry you'll be asked to speak, Sheila, but please don't go sticking up for me off your own bat. If my career depends on the word of a lying pip-squeak like that, then it's too bad.'

He was striding out and she allowed him to go. How could one condone this morning's horrid accusations with the man who had said, 'There are no indeterminate stages between wrong and right' . . . ? Just when everything promised to be so lovely this terrible business had to fall like blight upon their happiness. It didn't seem fair!

A scandal, of course, spreads like bindweed through the dining-room and into the wards. Martha Haley heard a garbled version, and only when she heard Mark's name did she prick up her ears and seek the truth. She was very sympathetic when discussing the business with the RMO's registrar, who was also a woman, and said, 'Poor, poor Mark!' with feeling.

'Why poor Mark?' asked Rose Honiton. 'I would have thought you'd have believed him against a mere student. We must stick together.'

'Well, of course I do. But—well, of course I do!' Martha avowed this in such a way that Rose was left wondering if there could be any truth in the student's statement after all. 'It's awful even to have it suggested that one is mixed up in drugs,' Martha went on apparently ingenuously. 'You know they do say that an addict desires to make others like him. It relieves his guilt.'

'You're not telling me Mark Leighton is an addict, Martha?'

The other looked pained. 'We're not discussing personalities, Rose. Just generalities. 'Bye for now.'

Martha still burned with anger and hatred when she remembered how Mark had rejected her advances. Instead of being appeased her hatred fanned hotter every day until she sometimes thought her head would burst with it. Now, with a weapon placed in her hands, she could hardly wait to strike.

★   ★   ★

Sheila found sleep elusive. The morning's events had upset her as though they had happened to her personally. She decided to read through part of Mark's thesis until Morpheus claimed her, and sat up in bed with the sheets of foolscap, closely written, in her hands. Mark had taken for his subject that most mysterious of human organs, the spleen. He had obviously studied and researched most thoroughly and had chapter headings describing surgical removal of the entire spleen and future prognosis and progress of people who had suffered splenectomy operations. Sheila read here and there haphazardly, at first, trying to make out Mark's longhand more than actually absorbing the facts. She still felt wide awake and so settled to read the chapter headed 'Effects of tropical diseases upon the spleen, in particular enlargement due to malarial infection, and prognosis.' The word 'enlargement' was still clearly discernible, but it had been crossed through and the word 'diminution' printed over. Sheila stared, for without being an expert she knew that an attack of malaria causes the spleen to almost double its size in some cases. What could Mark be thinking about when he had obviously made such a careful study of his subject, even to the point of injecting mice with malarial parasites and then removing their spleens for observation?

He must have been tired when he made such a correction in the script, or rather, mistake. She would mention it when they met and ask him what he meant by it. It was then sleep came to her eyes and she had to lay the manuscript down again. The dream was bad, though, and upsetting. She saw an unending series of doors all closing in Mark's face. He looked sad and turned to her, calling her name, but a door was between them, too, and she couldn't open it. She awoke making grunting noises of distress. It was a little after four p.m.

★   ★   ★

Martha Haley was beginning to conclude this was just not her day. Sir William had not come in until after three o'clock, having been delayed by an emergency thoroeaplasty in another hospital. Two of the recent post-operative patients had developed troubles which kept her tied to the ward; one was having a violent rigor during a blood transfusion, so this had needed to be halted; she was now watching the man who was on a saline drip, hoping for his colour to improve and his temperature to rise before continuing the transfusion proper. In the women's ward a woman had coughed and haemorrhaged from her wound. The house-surgeons had felt the lash of Martha's tongue today, even young Doane whose praises she had lately sung to Mark. He had always been a bit of a dumb-bell, actually, and inclined to hold to his opinions with the tenacity of a bulldog, whether his registrar agreed with them or not, which did not endear him to her one bit. She had used his name merely to antagonise Mark, unsettle him from the security of his assured niche in the ward. She had also felt sure of her own power with Sir William until the last couple of days. She was determined that he should oust Mark as she had once pushed him under his nose, but Sir William took more convincing than she had imagined. He had had time to assess the young man's qualities for himself, and in him he had found all the ingredients of a perfect lieutenant. One didn't find men of Mark's calibre every day and he couldn't understand Martha's sudden volte-face. He had rather brushed her off when she had laid this inefficiency at Mark's door, and that ... Apart from the fact that young women were all darlings, and when they had skills and brains as well, adorable poppets, they were as a sex wholly unpredictable, and he didn't care to try to understand their behaviour when it ran out of context.

Martha had been seething all day in

anticipation of seeing her boss. He appeared with a good-humoured boom at the patients nearest the door, always those who were most critically ill.

'Hello, my dears!' Men and women were all 'my dears' to Sir William, and this was the men's ward. 'I shall see you in just one moment when I've read what they say about you.'

He and Sister disappeared into the office and Martha joined them with a normal, 'Good afternoon, sir!' and a familiar, 'How's your gout?' to show that she knew him better than Sister.

'Fine, my dear. Fine. Ah, what have we here? Mr Oakley is reacting, is he? We can't have that with a haem count of only forty-six per cent, can we? Get on to the Department of Serology and tell them we want washed cells equivalent to three pints of AB positive, and that we want them instanter.' He looked up suddenly. 'I meant you, Miss Haley.'

Martha flushed. She had hoped Sister would go and then she could tell Sir William about the morning's shenanigans. She now hastened to obey. When the boss said jump, one jumped.

The ward round proceeded before she had another chance to speak to him alone, and then Sir William decided he had time for a cup of tea before moving on to see his private patients. Sister went to supervise the tea-making, to produce her own bone-china cups and get the tin of biscuits she kept in her locker. Martha said conversationally, 'Poor Mark got himself in a spot of bother this morning. It's all over the hospital.'

'He seduced Night Sister in the clinical room?' Sir William asked blandly. 'I've always hoped that would happen one of these days.'

'You will have your joke, sir.' Martha smiled thinly. 'It was more serious than that, however.'

'More serious than seduction? Good gracious! I'm all ears.'

'One of the students on duty said he had been supplied drugs by Mr Leighton; that he had paid him for them. The drugs were discovered to be missing from Casualty, too.'

'Do we keep cannabis resin in our drug cupboards, Martha? I can't think of any other drug I would care to pay for. At least with the good old hash one enjoys a state of euphoria for a while. But normal drugs are so dull and their only lasting effect is that they are extremely binding.' Sir William tapped the desk, looking genial at all his own jokes. 'Did I ever tell you about the chap who came to see me when I first moved into Harley Street?'

'Yes, you did, sir. He was an Irish navvy

and he said, "I haven't been for three weeks".'

'That's right.' Sir William refused to be silenced, however. 'Only *he* said, "Oi haven't bane for three wakes." I said—I was very obtuse—"Been where, my man?" and he actually blushed, all six foot three square of him, and muttered, "To the bathroom, Doctor. Oi can't go." And I said—oh, pathetic young man that I was!—"Well, don't worry. You look quite clean to me. Now let's talk about your health".'

Martha's laughter wanted to turn into a scream as Sister re-entered followed by a young nurse carrying the tray. Sir William settled himself and smiled all round. 'That's a nice young girl, Sister. Very shapely calves.'

'Yes, sir. The pity is she doesn't use them enough for my liking when she's on duty.'

'Oh, I do like these little tea-parties,' the consultant went on. 'All the lovely gossip. Now what were you telling me about this cannabis resin party, my dear?' he smiled encouragingly at Martha.

'I didn't mention cannabis resin, sir. That was your contribution. I told you Mark Leighton was involved in a drug racket with a student.'

'Oh, has that been proved, then, Miss Haley?' Sister asked quickly.

'Yes, has it?' demanded Sir William. 'I wouldn't like to think I was tried and condemned on a student's say-so alone. The young devils never reveal the true source of their supply, if they can help it, for fear of it being cut off. If Mark was blamed he's probably the last one who will be officially suspected.'

Martha felt she was losing ground rapidly.

'It does the ward no good to be involved in any internal hospital scandal,' she said virtuously. 'Supposing the papers get hold of it?'

'But who says they will? And newspapers are notoriously shy of being sued. Students are notorious little snirges. I was once a snirge. And I'll bet you, Martha, were a bitchy little snirge.'

'Sir, I don't know what a snirge is! You're always making up words. If you'll excuse me I'll go back to Mr Oakley and hear somebody talk sense for a change!'

This, in front of Sister, was unforgivable, and though Sir William's bland smile did not fade for an instant, his mind was busily ticking over and he thought, 'Martha's getting just a bit too big for her shoes. I'll have her over to dinner and sound her out about making a change. I think young Leighton might do very well here. I wonder just how heavily he trod on her pretty little toes?'

★   ★   ★

Sheila could have wept with disappointment when Mark did not appear on duty that night. She at first thought it must be something to do with the episode and accusation of the morning, but the man who did come on duty, a very large, handsome and hirsute Welshman by the name of Jones-Jones, not forgetting the hyphen, told her otherwise.

'Mark is temporarily under the weather with a temp and a head like an unexploded bomb,' he explained. 'The RMO asked me to stand in for one night as I'm just back from leave and fairly fresh. Fairly fresh,' he repeated with a leer, 'that's what the little dark-eyed damsel in Majorca called me!'

Dai Jones-Jones was one of the hospital's heart-throbs; he not only looked good but could sing like an opera star also; added to this he was athletic and upheld his hospital's honour on the rugby field and at cricket. The only reason he hadn't yet married was that he was a little bit too much in love with himself and hadn't enough admiration to spare for another.

Sheila wondered about Mark; why hadn't he sent a message himself that he wouldn't be

204

coming on duty? She imagined that right up to the last minute he had intended coming and then decided his efficiency was bound to be impaired. That was the only thing which would stop him; patients had to have one hundred per cent care and a man feeling under par couldn't give it.

Nurse Lewis was wandering about full of lugubrious humour and, surely enough, Matron had produced a relief nurse to help her. The two girls flitted about companionably, keeping the cubicles fresh and uncluttered and the medical staff supplied with coffee. It looked like being an amicable night, at least. Sheila eyed the volunteer students sharply for signs of unnatural stimulation. They were inclined to look away, embarrassed. Obviously they had heard what had occurred last night and maybe felt ashamed for the guilty one of their number.

Sheila had to hear of some of Dai Jones-Jones' many conquests. They were legion.

'I used to date that Haley woman,' he said at length. 'Now she was a real eye-opener if you like. I've always liked women to be cool, like beer. I thought Martha was as cool as cool until we went back to her flat. Do you know . . . ?' He hesitated to go into details as Sheila's eye daunted him. 'Well! A sonic boom has nothing on Martha when she's in the mood. I didn't fancy her so much after that, but I'd heard she could be very nasty, so I hung around her until she tired of me. Ah, Mark's on Sir William's firm too, isn't he? That means Martha approves of him. Now I wonder how far *he* went?'

Sheila didn't like this chatter very much. She stood up. 'Everybody doesn't have to kow-tow to Martha Haley,' she said shortly. 'Mark happens to be a chest man.'

'And Martha's a chest woman,' nodded Dai. 'What could be more obvious than that they discuss operational procedures together?'

'I think we have a customer,' said Sheila. 'I'll see to it.' She felt it was going to seem a very long night.

*   *   *

The regulars of the Crown hostelry eyed the stranger dubiously. He kept smiling and looking as though he was going to say 'Have the next one on me,' but he never quite got around to it, and his smile became vacuous and meaningless and the regulars stopped regarding him, thinking him to be a bit peculiar.

He was a bald, moon-faced little man, who, because of his baldness, looked older than his forty-three years. From the manner of his dress he could be a clerk or a small-time solicitor; he wore a stiff collar, a dark suit and a white shirt. The Crown was obviously not his local, for the regulars were mostly labouring types, typical working men who built houses or laid drains or clocked in at factories. They mopped down their beer by the pint and the little man sat at his table and smiled when the dart-players hit doubles and trebles, and took an occasional sip at his half of old and mild.

It wanted five minutes to closing time when the stranger approached the bar. Since finishing his half-pint he hadn't bought anything else and his smile had faded somewhat. He looked merely puzzled.

'Barman!' There was an immediate silence. Joe was always Joe, nobody called him barman.

'Yes, sir?' Joe was drawing last pints expertly. 'What kin I do fer you?'

'Do you know me?'

There was a guffaw nudged into silence.

'I don't know that I do, sir. Who are you?'

'I—I don't know. I'm afraid I don't know.'

'Well, sir, you shouldn't 'ave 'ad so many. You certainly 'aven't spent much 'ere.'

'I'm not drunk. I seem to have amnesia, or something.' There were gapes at this. 'I've lost my memory,' the stranger explained.

There was an uneasy silence. This was obviously a cod. Joe eyed the clock warily. Time was due to be called.

'Now why don't you just go 'ome, sir?' he pleaded.

'Because I don't know where to go. I'd have done it long ago. I thought somebody might have recognised me. Otherwise, what am I doing here?'

'Well, wot's wrong with 'ere?' Joe asked truculently.

'I don't mean that. A man goes into his own pub. Obviously this isn't my pub.'

'Ah we know you really lost your memory?' asked Red Harry. 'Ah we know you didn't walk out on your wife and family to be wi' your fancy piece, eh?'

There was more laughter, but Joe did not join in. The stranger did not at all fit this picture. He was no more a Romeo than Joe was the Aga Khan.

'Toime, gennelmen, *please!*' Joe roared. With the prospect of free entertainment it was difficult getting the crowd to leave. 'Now, sir, I must ask yer to leave or I'll 'ave ter call the police.'

The stranger sank down wearily at the same table where he had drunk his beer.

'Yes, please,' he requested civilly. 'Will you do that?'

The policeman greeted Sheila with a nod as she came forward.

'It could be a genuine case of amnesia,' he said, indicating the little bald man being led off by Nurse Lewis to a cubicle. 'I haven't been able to trip him. He has no papers or identification on him and his suit's off the peg from Burton's. All he remembers is sitting in this pub in Railway Road. He bought half a pint of beer, which he didn't like, and has three pounds sixty in his pocket. He doesn't seem to have been clubbed, or fallen heavily. His head isn't bruised or contused, and you can certainly see it all.'

Sheila said, 'I'll have a word with him and keep him for the psychiatrists in the morning.'

She had never met a case of amnesia before. She smiled at the little man and said, 'Mr— er—?' but he was not forthcoming and merely smiled back. 'I shall call you Mr X for the time being,' she said, filling in the required card. 'How do you feel in yourself?'

'Oh, perfectly well. All I feel is terrified, as though I'm locked in a dark room. I know there's a world out there, waiting, but I can't recall my place in it. It—it is rather terrible, you know.'

'Yes, Mr—er—I know it must be.' Sheila placed her hand on his arm reassuringly. 'You're in hospital now, however, and we'll look after you until you get out of this dark room. Does that make you feel any better?'

'Thank you. Are you a doctor?'

'Yes. This is the casualty department of St John's hospital.' No response. 'I'm going to ask you if you remember this or that, or try to jog your memory. I'm going to put you to sleep and make you comfortable until morning. I'm sure your people must be looking for you, and if I'm asked I can say you're here and safe.'

'If I *have* any people,' he said dully.

For the first time Sheila thought how terrible it must be to have lost not only one's identity but those of one's loved ones. How could one love the unknown? Supposing some crazed little woman came in shouting Albert, or Henry, and holding out her arms, would the response be a blank stare of incomprehension? How did one act in cases like these?

Dai was most interested to hear about Mr X, and of course he had a story to tell.

'I heard of a man, once, who sounds like your Mr X. He was middle-aged, paunchy, mediocre and a minor civil servant by profession. He was widowed, waited a respectable time and then married a cracker, a big Amazon of a woman, blonde, busty and dim. He was the sort who played chess and she—well! He wandered into the police station after being missing for two weeks, unshaven but quite happy. Didn't know who he was and didn't want to know. His wife traced him, of course, but he refused to acknowledge her, even, or couldn't. He didn't regain his memory and his wife was eventually granted a divorce. She was the sort who needs a man in her life. Then one day he announced that he remembered everything, though funnily enough he also remembered he was free, without prompting. He married a nice little middle-aged nondescript, like himself, and they lived happily ever after.'

'Now I know it's a story,' said Sheila.

'You doubt my word? Ask Bill Verreker.'

'He's another,' Sheila said ambiguously, shrugging off Dai's arm which had somehow come to rest on her shoulder. 'Look, as we're not busy would you like to go and lie down?'

'You mean there's nothing doing before I even start?'

'I mean exactly that.'

'I didn't know you were spoken for.'

'That's beside the point. I mean we're on duty and should comport ourselves with dignity. I'm not an insatiable blonde, and after almost a week of this I'm very tired.'

'Scout's honour, hands off. *You* go and lie down.'

Sheila was tempted. It wasn't like being with Mark, being content to watch his comings and goings and catching his eye occasionally. Dai went off shortly afterwards to repair a cracked plaster which was causing a sufferer some movement in a broken limb and, therefore, pain. She thought about what he had told her of Martha Haley. Had there been some interest between Martha and Mark? She was in a state where she couldn't imagine any woman not loving Mark, and yet it was pain to picture another in his arms. Also she already knew him well, knew how even his passion had to submit to will. He was strict about his own behaviour and expected others to be the same. He would always take some living up to both professionally and morally; looseness in a woman would make him positively ill.

Around midnight there was a spurt of activity and both doctors were kept busy removing splinters, stitching cuts, painting painful cavities in teeth and replacing a dislocation. A coloured woman came in complaining of earache. Sheila looked within and saw that the drum was indeed inflamed a little.

'I think a shot of penicillin and wait and see,' she smiled reassuringly. 'When are you expecting the baby?' It was obvious that the woman was pregnant.

'Next month, I think. I never know for sure.'

This sounded like the voice of experience.

'How many children have you?' Sheila asked.

'This will be my eighth. I have one every year I live with my husband. The two years he was in England, before we join him, I don't have any babies. That was good.'

'Why don't you ask to be sterilised?'

'Sterilised? No, sir! My grandmom she had thirteen children, ten died. My mamma had nine children and five died. I'm going to have all the children God sends and all going to live. Times is getting better.'

'I'll go and prepare the injection,' said Sheila, having visions of one very large family by the time the woman was forty. The two nurses were bandaging and Dai was extracting a recalcitrant milk tooth. As she returned with the hypodermic in a kidney dish she heard her patient call, 'Doctah! Are you there?'

'Yes?' Sheila stared as she edged between the drawn curtains. The woman had pushed down the blue blanket covering her and between her knees was a little copper-coloured bundle. 'I'm sorry, Doctor, but it just came.'

'Your baby?' Sheila nearly had a most unprofessional fit. 'Without any pains?' she asked.

'Well, I been so conscious of my ear all day I never gave a thought to anything else. I'm sorry to be such a nuisance.'

All the others doing unimportant jobs were rallied to perform what was necessary in sustaining the little life which had appeared so miraculously amongst them. The baby was a girl, a healthy six-and-a-half-pounder, and it was given the name of Sheila there and then by the grateful mother.

'But I didn't do *anything*,' Dr Devaney protested.

'You did indeed. D'you know my ear's quite better? It doesn't hurt any more.'

It was then Sheila remembered that the injection had never been given, and smiled to herself.

★   ★   ★

Casualty was always covered by the night staff until eight a.m., but when the cleaners arrived at six-thirty it always looked like the end of the stint and flagging spirits usually revived as the pangs of hunger awakened. At seven-thirty Mark walked into the department and

214

Sheila ran to meet him, her countenance aglow, convinced that he was going to take her in his arms. He did, of course, quite spontaneously, and then Dai's voice came irrepressibly, 'Hi! Hi!' and the magic moment was ended.

'So that's why I got the frozen mitt all night,' he ruminated.

'Has he been bothering you?' Mark asked, making a playful pass at Dai's chin.

'No, actually,' Sheila smiled, 'we've been too busy having birthdays and what have you. Mark, how are you?'

'Oh, fair to middling after a good night's sleep,' he told her, tucking her arm in his. 'It was an attack of hay fever. I simply couldn't open my wretched eyes. You must think I'm a bit of an invalid one way and another.'

'If that's all, I'll cope with you.'

'Brazen woman! I haven't popped the question yet.'

But his eyes told her it was only a matter of time, that it was an occasion to draw out and enjoy, like a seven-course dinner.

'I came to tell you I have some business to wrap up, today, so I won't see you until tonight. Now that I have my car things are so much easier.'

'I'm glad. But you must get back in time to have a couple of hours' rest.'

215

'Madam,' he concurred with a small bow, kissed her hand and was gone.

'Yon's a good lad,' remarked Dai. 'Is it serious with you?'

'I hope so.' She felt she was counting her chickens and Dai was a gossip. 'We knew each other in medical school, but there's nothing settled, of course.'

'Well, if you've any respect for a woman scorned, don't settle things just now, for your own sake.'

She pondered her colleague's words. He seemed to think that no one could escape Miss Haley's attentions whom she desired. If they resisted her there was the alternative of her revenge.

'I'm sure Dai exaggerates terribly,' she pondered. 'Miss Haley is so attractive she must have hundreds of admirers. Even she knows she can't have everybody or force anyone to love her.'

'Well, well, well!' Dr Merritt, the senior casualty officer on day duty, arrived, rubbing his large hands together. 'Another day, another dollar. I suppose you're all loth to leave me?'

Sheila's 'Good morning, Doctor', came from way up the corridor where he had a back view of her disappearing fast.

'Now that,' philosophised Dr Merritt, 'was

216

a beautiful conversation if you like. Come on, Jonesy! Not you, too. You can take me through the log, you lazy so-and-so. In any case it's bangers for breakfast and they're nicely rubberised to a turn!'

★　　★　　★

Sheila's mother was giving a bridge tea. She looked at her daughter in some irritation.

'Really, Sheila, you never advise me when you're coming! How can we chat when I'm in the thick of things like this? I only have them here once a month. You *are* the limit!'

'Do you know, Mother, you have the most hectic social life of anybody I know? When your friends are not here you're bridging at their homes, and then you have your committees and your Council work. I have to nip out whenever I can and you're always busy. I accept the fact, now, that whenever I come home I'm a hindrance.'

'Oh, what a terrible thing to say! You simply don't understand me, how I must keep going with something or other. Your father didn't understand me, and you're exactly like him.'

'Now, Mother, I was only teasing. It's good for you to keep busy. You don't know how many middle-aged women do nothing but

217

moan about having nothing to occupy them. They usually suffer from hypochondria. You go back to your play. I shall help myself to a cup of tea.'

The garden in June was a mass of roses, delphiniums and hollyhocks; the French windows stood open and Sheila wandered outside balancing a cup of tea and a plate of cakes; she sat on the grass by the sun-dial and tried to think about herself and Mark, the miracle of this past week. She also thought about Bruce and hoped he wasn't too upset.

From the house came the bridge calls: 'Two hearts', 'Three clubs', and her mother's voice, conclusively, 'Four hearts', and then a murmur of no-bids.

'I'm dummy,' announced Mrs Devaney, joining her daughter. 'I should really have called a small slam, but Jean Mathers is such a fool she's bound to lead into their clubs. Now, how is my dear Bruce?'

'Mother,' Sheila had to get this moment over, 'that's all over. I came specially to tell you. I have to go soon, I'm on night duty.'

'All over? Bruce and you? But it was an ideal match. All my life I've worried about you, wondered what foolishness you would make of yours, but when I met Bruce I thought, "My darling's safe. He's a good, good man".'

'Mother, a man doesn't only have to be good. One must also be in love with him.'

'What rubbish is this? Being in love is adolescent nonsense. After the first year you look for solidarity and decent human qualities. Bruce had them all.'

'Mother—!'

'I suppose you imagine you are "in love" with somebody else?'

'I do, yes.' All the magic had gone, however, killed by Mrs Devaney's experienced, firm objections.

'And is he going to marry you? Can he hold a candle to Bruce, who could give you a nice home and security and a ready-made job?'

'Mother, I came to tell you, and I've told you my news. I don't, however, have to ask your permission either to love or marry whomsoever I will. I have to go now, and I think they're calling for you.'

She was upset, however, as she drove back to the hospital. It was true that mother and daughter were chalk and cheese in so many respects. There was only a truce when Sheila conformed to her mother's ideas of how a daughter should behave. The battles had been prolonged throughout her medical training; Mrs Devaney did not like professional women; she had objected to Sheila's friendship with Mark simply because he was poor and unestablished. What she would say when she knew it was Mark again did not bear thinking about. She would be rude to Mark, bring Bruce's name into the conversation and be generally obstructive wherever she could.

'We have to be sure enough for it not to matter,' Sheila told herself. She was sure, but one cannot be certain for another.

Mark's day also had gone somewhat agley.

He had been visiting Australia, New Zealand and Canada Houses with a view to gathering the 'gen' regarding emigration. He had been quite set in his mind that now a second and more favourable chance of happiness with Sheila had come his way, he wanted only the very best for them both. To be Martha's puppet he was not at all inclined; if Sir William heeded his fair registrar then Mark might as well leave all he had worked for and look elsewhere. He would not have Sheila, as his wife, anywhere where that harpy could get her claws into her.

Everyone welcomed his enquiries—at first. Then, in general discussion, the fact emerged that he had once suffered an attack of poliomyelitis. Then his interviewers became extremely apologetic but adamant. Emigrants were required not only to be, but to have been, one hundred per cent fit all their lives.

'But I *am* fit,' Mark insisted. 'I can get

medical confirmation. Good lord, I couldn't do my work if I wasn't fit!'

The 'I'm sorry, Doctor' became sick with repetition. They were sure he could do his work, but if one exception to the rule was made then the odd crock or two would slip in and crumble the whole edifice of controlled emigration.

He turned away disappointed, disillusioned and frustrated. To have to work in this country, where competition was so great, now appeared dull and unenterprising. At one stage of his career he would have placed British medicine supreme in the whole world; America had the dollars, but Britain had the men and the brains and medical schools second to none. Also this country, which was his, had nursed him through his illness, rehabilitated him and given him back his job without it costing him one penny, except in time lost and years gone to waste. He had pictured sailing away into the sun somewhere, with Sheila, and now that this was denied him he could see only a general greyness; the silver lining was elusive at that moment.

He, too, went home to see his mother. She was just home from work and looked at him uncertainly yet with irrepressible joy.

'Mark, what would you say if I told you I might be getting married again? Would you

221

mind?'

'Mind?' he looked overcome. 'You're kidding, sweetie. Who would have an old hag like you to wife?'

She tweaked his nose. This had always been the basis of their relationship, more brother and sister than mother and son. They each got on with their lives independently of the other.

'He's my boss and he thinks I'll do, anyhow. I thought I'd better tell you, at least. Whether you approve or not won't make the slightest difference. Now tell me you've found the only girl in the world and I'll be happy.'

Mark couldn't loosen his tongue about his own affairs, however. With emigration denied him he could see other things failing to come to fruition, too.

'You mean it's catching, this thing?' he joked. 'It goes through families like Roman noses and bandy legs?'

'You'll have to be thinking about settling down, my bright boy, because I'm young enough to have a little brother for you and then I'll be too busy to sew on your buttons and darn your socks.'

He did a bit of mental arithmetic, cocked one eyebrow and smiled. 'Mother, you were not a child bride. You're not codding *me*. You may only look forty, but you're fifty-two, and if you have a baby it will be a real achievement and we'll put the flags out and write to *The Times*. Now be your age and put the kettle on, Polly, do!'

CHAPTER TWELVE

'It must have been his promotion that did it,' the modest, plump little woman whimpered softly, looking afraid, not seeing the elegantly grey-carpeted room which was Dr Eisinger's office. 'You see we come from the North; with me you can tell, but Walter always tried to cover up his accent. Not many people could tell Walter was born in Salford, I can tell you, and he allus had gentlemanly instincts, didn't like dirty hands. Nothing like that. So he got a job in an office; it didn't pay much, but we managed and we was happy. Walter used to play bowls and I would watch. That was our pleasure. That and the test matches. When they came to Old Trafford Walter and me would queue for hours. We used to think of Washbrook and Ikin as our own—well, northerners are like that. They're one big family. We had a nice little garden, out in the suburbs we lived, you know; and people walking by would admire Walter's roses and carnations. He would tell where he got the plants or give them cuttings. It was really very nice and pleasant. Then there was one of these take-overs and Walter's firm was swallowed up. Hundreds lost their jobs, but Walter was told he'd be kept on, and promoted, if he could handle the job and move south at an increased salary. Well, it didn't sound at all bad put like that. We sold our little house and moved down south, here, but we had a fit when we discovered the price of houses. A three-bedroomed terraced one was all we could afford, and it only has a small area and a shrub or two and *no bathroom*. Then, down here, nobody speaks to you, and Walter missed his garden. His wages didn't seem to go nowhere, either and at work he was a funny little nobody they all laughed at. Last night when he didn't come home my first thought was that he'd jumped in the river, but my Walter isn't a coward, and when I thought again I knew he wouldn't do that to me. So it seems that with one thing and another—'

The specialist put his hand on the other's arm.

'Thank you, my dear, you've been very frank and I understand perfectly. The human mind is something of which our knowledge is still very limited and sometimes it just withdraws from life, shutting all the doors of memory, which may not be such a bad thing as it may stop someone from committing an act of violence against himself, such as jumping in the river, which you mentioned. We'll go and see Walter now, but I've warned you what to expect, so don't be surprised.'

Walter Oldenshaw was not ill, so he was sitting in the dayroom of the psychiatric wing at St John's, wearing a perplexed frown and riffling through a pile of periodicals and magazines. His eyes lit up when he saw the doctor, but the woman, his wife, he ignored completely.

'Doctor, I found a picture in a book here. I seem to think my house is like this.' He displayed the picture of a pleasant little semi-detached villa on a corner with an expanse of floriferous garden. 'I can tell you the name of that rose, it's McGredy's Yellow. I'm sure I had one.'

'Half a dozen, Walter,' said the woman, 'and you're quite right. That could be our house.'

The doctor said, ventriloquist-wise, 'Slowly, slowly, and you may catch a monkey,' and left them together.

More than an hour later they both appeared in his office escorted by a beaming Sister. Walter was dressed. The pucker had left his brow.

'Well, Doctor, thank you all, but

everything came back. This is the little woman, by the way, my wife, Elizabeth.'

'We have met,' nodded Dr Eisinger. 'What's happening now?'

'Well, Walter isn't going back to *that* place. Sister said you might give us a letter . . . ?'

'Certainly,' he smiled. 'Mr Oldenshaw should go back north. I shall recommend that.'

'. . . And we have to sell the place we're in and then try to find one with a garden similar to our old house.'

'That should be a mutual pleasure.'

'Then Walter has to find another job.'

'Ah. That may not be too easy, but—'

'Don't you worry, Doctor,' Walter said confidently, 'I shall find something. There's only the two of us and my Elizabeth will buckle to and help, if she has to. There's just one thing—when I was brought here last night, there was a very sweet young girl who said she was a doctor . . .'

'Oh, yes, that's our Dr Devaney. As you say, Mr Oldenshaw, a very sweet girl.'

'Will you tell her I—got out, and will you say thanks, for me?'

'I will indeed.'

'Come on, love,' Elizabeth Oldenshaw took Walter's arm with the comfortable assurance of habit and familiarity, 'we're going home.'

Sheila could sense that Mark was somewhat withdrawn that evening and so didn't press him into conversation. Having known him previously she was well aware that he was a complex person; there were times when he wanted to gambol through Elysian fields and others when he shut himself behind barriers with his thoughts. This was one of those times, and she knew there is nothing more irritating than not being allowed to be alone even when one is in company.

It was a night busy without being dramatic. There was a crop of fractures and a couple of car accidents where the only damage was caused by flying glass, fortunately, and the victims looked far worse than they were. The case of the night was a scalded child, though how such a thing could happen at two in the morning was difficult to comprehend.

As the early hours trod leaden-footed one after the other, Sheila finally became somewhat restive.

'Mark,' she accosted him, 'are you upset about anything?'

He shrugged slightly. 'Sorry. Have I been like a broody hen? No, not really upset, simply preoccupied.'

'Oh. I had noticed after almost seven hours of it.'

'I'm sorry, Sheila.' He patted her arm almost avuncularly. 'I haven't been very attentive, I know, but you would understand if you knew.'

'Very well. Tell me,' she urged.

'I—er—want you to forget the other night, Sheila, and carry on as though it had never been.'

'I don't understand, Mark.' Her eyes were large and questioning.

'Sheila, I'm not free to ask you to be my wife. My feelings haven't changed, but there are difficulties at present.'

She caught her breath in some relief, 'Well, Mark, your feelings are what are important to me. There's no hurry for anything else.'

'I think it's wrong to tie you down without definite prospects. No matter what you say that's what split us asunder the last time.'

Pride, the intruder between lovers, spoke next through her lips.

'You're under no obligation to me, Mark. Would you rather we didn't meet?'

'Well, I finish my contract here next week and submit my thesis, then I have my leave. I'll probably be travelling about a bit and . . .'

'There's no need to go on, Mark. You know where I'll be until the end of February next.'

Tears smarted behind her lashes. Once before she had watched him go off and leave her behind. They both knew well how that had felt.

He said in a softer voice, 'I've upset you. I'm sorry. This week has been wonderful, Sheila, but it isn't all that easy just joining the ends. You know where *I'll* be tomorrow if you care to drop in.'

This reminded her that the six nights of their Casualty stint were coming to an end. There would be no more of those coffee breaks, searching out one another's pasts and leading up to falling in love again. Something had happened which had made Mark pause in making advances to her; it was as though he had suffered some shock, lost his mental assuredness.

They went their ways eventually with scarcely a word. It was too painful to be casual when love wanted simply to love and not count the cost.

Mark was not enjoying his breakfast. The kippers were salty and tasted as though they had been too long in plastic bags. Harold Doane tapped him on the shoulder. 'Mark, Miss Haley would appreciate a word with you before you go off anywhere. She'll be on the ward at nine.'

'OK,' Mark told the other. He wondered

what Martha wanted with him and was taken aback when he found out.

'Mark!' the lovely face was all softness and apology. 'I wanted to see you and wondered if you'd come. You've finished your night stint, haven't you?'

'Yes, Miss Haley, I have.'

'Martha to you,' she smiled, 'and don't worry that I'm going to try to eat you—again.' She laughed openly at his expression. 'I was angry and humiliated, but, as you said, we're both adults and I couldn't keep up a stupid feud with you. Would you—shake?' She held out a long, slim hand. He had always admired her hands. He took it and gripped it briefly in his own.

'I'm glad that's over, Martha. No hard feelings, I assure you.'

'Where are you spending your short leave?'

'On my wee boat. I'll be back Sunday night ready for the usual grind on Monday.'

'I'll see you then,' she told him. 'Oh, I wonder if you would take my keys while I pop down to my room? Mr Henry—you remember Mr Henry?—may require some digitalis if he has pain before I get back. I won't be long, but I do like to think there's somebody reliable in charge while I'm gone.'

She was back within ten minutes, profuse in her gratitude and urging him to have a lovely time.

'Get plenty of rest, Mark. You look really exhausted.'

He was just beginning to realise how tired he was, but he was determined to get down to Marlow before taking to his bunk. There the river noises were soothing to him; he was sure he would sleep like a baby. His small case was standing on his bed in his room already containing pyjamas and a couple of shirts. He threw in his shaving kit—that, too, was a job which could wait—looked around for a couple of paperback books, stuffed several notes into his wallet and set forth jingling the keys of the Triumph wondering why he didn't feel very happy about anything.

*   *   *

After a couple of hours' sleep Sheila decided it was a pity to waste more of such a lovely day in bed. She could do so many things she had wanted to, such as running down to Brighton to see Mavis, her friend of medical school days, or go and enjoy a shopping spree in the nearby Saturday market, or even go into the country and breath fresh air, unwinding tensions with nature's aids and examples. Whoever saw a tense cow, or felt giddy at the sight of a leisurely-turning water-wheel? She never once considered going down to Marlow. She was hurt and felt rebuffed and somehow aged, as though she had lived a lifetime in one short week.

She finally decided to start the typing of Mark's thesis. This was something she had offered to do out of common friendship and when it was done would be a load off both his mind and hers.

The typewriter clicked away and she became engrossed, then she came to one of those crossings-out where something quite alien had been superimposed. Whatever was Mark thinking about? Even she knew his first thoughts had been correct on the subject, she who wasn't even a fledged doctor yet, let alone writing a thesis for her MD. She left a blank and, a few paragraphs further on, came to another questionable statement. She gave up in consternation. She couldn't proceed without Mark verifying that he had meant to write such things. It was then that she decided to go down to Marlow and settle the matter once and for all. Her heart told her this was what she had wanted to do all along, and by the time she was in her little car she was singing softly to herself.

Sir William Bender was met by his house-surgeons at the end of the corridor leading to the wards. He was bland and pink and shining, like a well-fed porker.

'Where's Miss Haley?' he wanted to know.

'Sir, there's been some trouble,' Doane said eagerly. 'We've had a raid on the drug cupboard. I'm afraid the police . . .'

'You don't mean to say police are on the ward?'

'Well, in the office, sir. The RMO and the hospital administrator are there as well. Miss Haley is with them.'

'I sincerely hope somebody is looking after my patients,' Sir William said drily, 'and I shall want to know who was careless enough to—'

Martha was looking tearful and *distraite*, but the consultant noticed that her beauty was unimpaired; she did not look blotched as a woman does suffering genuine grief.

'Oh, Sir William, this is terrible!' she greeted him.

'Has Mr James Bond visited us, or something?' he asked with heavy humour. 'You, Doane, and you, Camilla'—this in a softer tone to the junior—'go and do some work. There are quite enough of us here. Now'—he had immediately taken charge, like the leader of the pack—'who is going to tell me all about it, whatever it is?'

'Oh, sir,' said Martha, haltingly, 'I blame myself. I shouldn't have left the ward.'

'But you did?' prompted Sir William.

Martha turned away, apparently overcome, and the RMO, who was in charge of all drugs supplied to the wards, took over.

'It appears that Mr Leighton came to the ward for a chat with Miss Haley, Sir William, before going off on short leave after night duty. While he was here, Miss Haley asked him to take over while she went to change her duty coat, which was slightly blood-stained. She left the keys with Mr Leighton, in case one of the patients asked for his digitalis, which was due. She then took over again and Mr Leighton went off about his own business. There followed the usual Saturday morning stock-taking of drugs when it was discovered there was a considerable discrepancy of both phenobarbitone and preludine, which were not listed as having been drawn. Sister's key had never left her person, and it was then Miss Haley remembered handing over for a short time to Mr Leighton. She was agitated, naturally, and went to see if he was still on the premises, hoping he could perhaps explain the discrepancy. He had left, however, and so she called me and reported the facts.'

'As we couldn't trace Mr Leighton,' said Dr Thornbull, the Administrator, 'we took the liberty of looking in his room for possible information. We found the missing drugs in the pocket of a mackintosh hanging behind the door. That is when we asked the police to come.'

'You can't possibly suspect Mark Leighton of filching drugs?' hooted Sir William.

'There was that student accusation the other day,' said the RMO, 'and now the same type of drugs, both sedative and stimulant, are involved afresh. We naturally want to get to the bottom of the business.'

'Well, nobody so guilty could be so clumsy,' said the consultant. 'He's left with the keys to the drug cupboard in his hands for ten minutes, during which he takes—as you put it, Wilkie—drugs of a similar type to those found on a stupid boy a couple of days ago. He then takes these to his room, puts them openly in a pocket hanging behind—I have no doubt—an unlocked door and goes off knowing there's going to be panic stations when stock is taken that very day. Such a man isn't a crook, he's a damned fool, and Leighton is no fool.'

Martha was not sobbing so much now as grinding her teeth.

'Then how did the drugs get there, sir?' she asked him.

'Planted on him, my dear girl. It's plain as a pike-staff. Somebody's been very naughty, and I don't intend jumping to conclusions. As

I have a round to do would you all excuse me, please?'

'Certainly,' the RMO said coldly. He thought the whole business rather odd himself, but the drug scare was too real not to be taken seriously by such as he. It was a police matter to ask pertinent questions and get to the bottom of the unpleasant business. He would be as glad as anybody to have young Leighton cleared of the smear of this particular tar-brush.

'By the way,' Sir William turned in the doorway, 'if you want Mr Leighton he's bound to be down at Marlow. He has some sort of a boat there. He has probably gone to get a bit of peace, but you gentlemen will no doubt put an end to that.' He nodded at the detectives, who didn't quite know how to take him, and completely ignored Martha, who had dutifully tacked herself on to him.

*   *   *

Marlow is a beautiful little town at any season of the year but on a sunny June day with the gardens a riot of colour and the river shining under a blue heaven, to its beauty is added an attraction that is almost irresistible.

Sheila found the river a large place chock-a-block with craft of all descriptions. Those that

236

were not lying at their moorings were gliding, being rowed or propelled along in both directions. Looking for one small cabin cruiser was akin to seeking a needle in a haystack. She had walked half a mile down the towpath before she came upon the *Lady Verity*. She was lying in a mooring by a colourful-looking little tavern with continental window-blinds and mushrooming coloured umbrellas. She was rocking gently in the wash caused by passing boats. Her deck was miniscule, there was about room for one deckchair. Sheila, after jumping down to that deck and finding the impetus almost took her into the water, paused to get her breath and find her river legs. It was then she saw the cabin door was wide open: she looked within to see Mark asleep on his bunk, his upper half naked, lean and muscular. She descended a couple of brass-edged steps and sat down, feeling a little shy, now, of the whole adventure. He might be angry, or embarrassed or—worst of all—simply dismayed by her appearance.

The cabin was surprisingly capacious, taking in, as it did, the full draught of the boat. There was the bunk, which obviously folded away when not in use, a fixed table and a bench seat, a curtained corner, which was probably a shower-cubicle, and a small galley at the rear. Sheila could imagine any man loving such a trim little hideaway. The rocking was soothing, too. She quickly became conscious that she had had only a couple of hours' sleep and experimentally closed her eyes to see what would happen.

'Sheila, love ... ?' The voice came from a long way off and she opened leaden lids to behold Mark, in a towelling robe now, shaking her gently awake. 'How long have you been here?'

'I arrived about one o'clock.'

'It's a quarter to four now ...'

She didn't want to wake up to reality, the dream had been too sweet. If she closed her eyes again she might recapture ... and then the dream came true and Mark was crushing her to his chest with little explosions of pleasure and delight.

'You came,' he said, and kissed her long and lingeringly. 'You adorable creature! You came.'

'Mark'—she surfaced breathlessly—'I must be honest with you. I came to discuss your thesis with you. I was working on it. But having an excuse was all I needed—all my pride needed. I thought if you didn't want me I had a perfectly valid reason for being here. But I'm so glad I didn't need it.'

'We'll have to find excuses for not being

together in future, darling. I had my priorities all wrong. Here I was with my fine car and my boat, and the one thing I really wanted was missing. Having the others made it glaringly obvious.'

'Why did you try to put me off, Mark? What went wrong yesterday?'

'You know I had this idea about emigrating? I thought we would both go, find a good life together. I was going to bring back all the literature, brochures, forms and things and put it to you this very day. But they turned me down out of hand.'

'Because of the polio?'

'Yes. I felt for a time as though somebody had sprung the trap and I was dangling in space. I have to think again now.'

'Mark, *I'm* not disappointed because I never anticipated emigrating. I don't suppose the Commonwealth is too keen on taking raw doctors like me, in any case. I need a lot more experience.'

'D'you know, the fact that they questioned my fitness made me question it myself. I began to think, how do I know there won't be ill effects as I get older? Might my children be affected? I'd concluded I was a crock last evening.'

'Mark, you know that's not so. Thousands of people are doing normal jobs of work who

239

once had polio.'

'And none of them are able to emigrate,' he reminded her.

'So what? When I see a lovely little retreat such as you have here, I ask myself what's wrong with Britain? May I come again?'

'Look!' he said. He reached up and tugged at the wall over his bunk. With a creak another bunk came down. 'Married quarters,' he announced, and added wickedly, 'not that it's an ideal arrangement.' He pushed the second bunk back again. 'Come and try this one, just for size.' They sank down happily together and the next few minutes passed most enjoyably. Voices calling from the towpath suddenly intruded, however.

'Dr Leighton?' someone said officiously, knocking on the cabin roof.

'What the—?' Mark looked out. 'Come aboard if you want me,' he invited, as Sheila straightened her ruffled hair. 'Is somebody ill? Has there been an accident?'

'We're policemen, Doctor. Detective-Sergeant Warne and Constable Hoode. We would like some information from you to help us in our enquiries.'

'Yes?' asked Mark. He saw the Sergeant obviously questioning his attire, putting two and two falsely together when he saw Sheila in the cabin.

'This is Dr Devaney, gentlemen. She came to deliver some documents to me.'

'May we speak in front of the lady, sir?'

'Well, so long as it's decent,' Mark joked. He couldn't seriously believe the police were after him.

'We're enquiring after missing hospital drugs, sir. Can you help us at all?'

'Oh, that,' said Mark, misunderstanding. 'I thought all that had been tidied away. I never dreamed they'd call you chaps in.'

'It *is* a criminal offence, sir, procuring drugs either for resale or your own use.'

'I'm aware of that. Sheila, did you know you can't raid the drug cupboard and flog its contents?'

'Every doctor knows that,' Sheila said flatly.

'Then perhaps you could explain, Dr Leighton, how certain drugs came to be found in your room today?'

Mark looked up sharply.

'Who's been searching my room?' he demanded.

'Well, sir, the drugs were missing and you had had access . . .'

'I don't know what the devil you're talking about. I must be dense or something. Put it into words of one syllable if you can.'

'You were temporarily left in charge of

Ward Alpha this morning, and thereafter certain drugs were found to be missing. The young lady, I may add, was most upset. She insisted that there must be an explanation.'

'What young lady?'

The sergeant looked at his constable's notes. 'Name of Haley,' he said.

'Martha!' snapped Mark, tightening his lips. 'The kiss of Judas!' His eyes blazed. 'Sheila, go back to the hospital.'

'But—'

'I said go back! Get out of here! I don't want you involved in all this pig-swill. I'll probably be along later, in handcuffs. Get back and take this with you.' He slapped the envelope containing the thesis into her arms. 'When I'm struck off, reading that may amuse you.'

'Mark, I—'

'Or throw it in the river,' he said harshly. 'It's only six months' research, hopes and dreams. I'm fated never to get my MD. These gentlemen'—he waved at the detectives—'have practically convinced me.'

★   ★   ★

Sheila was so unhappy when she awoke on Sunday morning that she wanted to die. The fact that the police had been called into the hospital's affairs was no secret. Many-tongued rumour informed her that Mark Leighton had been suspended from duty pending enquiries.

She knew she mustn't seek him out. He would be as easy to approach as an elephant with toothache. She racked her brains wondering what she could do, for Mark was not guilty of any crime, as those who really knew him must be convinced. It was equally obvious that where there had been a crime there must be a criminal. Therefore, who was it? What had Mark meant by 'the kiss of Judas'?

Sheila finally decided to work on the thesis. The doubtful statements she would leave out to include later, making a full list of them. It was so odd that these were all second thoughts, having been written over true facts originally set down. She was determined that the thesis should be presented even though she sent it in herself, on Mark's behalf. There was a lot of effort in it and it would eventually be a most impressive medical test.

As she worked, having made sure no one had been on night duty on either side of her, and so would not be upset by the clacking of the typewriter, she began to have an uneasy suspicion that the manuscript had been interfered with by an outsider. Didn't Mark say he would have to collect it from Miss Haley to give to her, and would he have read it through again himself first? Of course not. The trusting soul must be so sick of it by now that he would have sent it to a typist just as it was, and a normal typist, without knowledge of medical terms, would have typed what was written without question. It was just possible that Mark, collecting the pristine pages, would be content to string them together and dispatch them; or, if he did spot the dubious statement, would be thoroughly outraged, probably with the typist.

So convinced did she become that Miss Haley was behind all that was happening to Mark that she made enquiries if Sir William Bender would be in that day. She was told that Sir William only came in on Sundays when one of his patients was very ill. There was such a patient in Beta Ward, and Sir William had said he would call in about midday and stay for lunch.

Armed with the thesis, Sheila lay in wait. The consultant arrived in his Daimler at ten past twelve and spent twenty minutes on the ward. He then came out accompanied by Martha and one of the house-surgeons, but after a few minutes' conversation he sent them back and continued on his way down the corridor towards the senior residents' sitting-room, alone.

Sheila popped out at him looking small and

feeling very shy.

'Sir William, please would you give me a minute of your time?'

'My dear, are you lost? Are you trying to find a ward? I'm sorry, but this place confuses me, too, and I only know the way from my own ward.'

'No, sir, I'm not lost. I—I work here. I'm doing my internship.'

'Oh, bless you! And you want to know what the chances are of joining my firm? Very good, my dear. Very good. I incline to pretty little fillies. When they lend you to a surgeon, ask to be lent to me. If you give me your name I'll arrange it.'

'Sir, I'm sorry, but would you allow me to speak? It—it's very important.'

'There, I'm such an egotistical brute! I think everybody is dying to be a thoracic surgeon. There's a great future in it though, my dear, if you should be at a loss. Now, what is it, then?'

'I'm a—a friend of Mr Leighton's, sir. I want to talk to you about him.'

Sir William's countenance clouded.

'Now, my dear, that's awkward, because the whole nasty business is out of my hands. I personally think it's a lot of baloney, which Mark will no doubt effectually prove for himself, but until the hospital holds its

245

enquiry, I am powerless to speak.'

'This is Mark's thesis, Sir William. I wonder if you would just read one page of it?'

'Well, what good . . . ?'

'It will only take a minute, sir.'

The consultant began to read almost irritably; he wanted his pre-lunch sherry with the RSO, who was no doubt awaiting him, and he was being held up by this chit of a girl who didn't even admit to wanting to join his firm. Half-way down the page, however, he stopped and read a sentence again.

'That's a barmy thing to say,' he muttered. 'What's Mark thinking of?'

'I have made a list of eighteen other barmy things he has apparently said, sir. But of course he didn't really say them. The manuscript came directly to me from Miss Haley. It seems she wants to hurt Mark in every possible way for some reason.'

'Yes, I would agree the supposed corrections are in Martha's scribble. I see it often enough. I would think she did this just to annoy, though it's a silly, mindless way of doing it. However, let us tax her with it.'

'Would you do it yourself, sir? If it was me, I would hate a stranger witnessing my discomfiture.'

'You're a nice little thing. You've got a kind heart. Wait for me here.'

He returned with a steely look in his normally mild blue eyes.

'Of course she denied tampering with the manuscript, at first, until I said we had better invite the police to give an opinion, seeing that they were swarming all over the building. Then she admitted it, and I invited her to come down and see the RMO, and clear up another matter which was just as silly as some of these statements. She is wondering how much I know and how much I'm simply guessing, but you and I had better call and see the RMO and tell him what a fool he's making of himself just lately.'

Sheila thought they better hadn't say that, exactly, but she was beginning to discover that Sir William thought himself a bit of a card and liked an audience. She played up by trotting along at his heels to the RMO's house, in the hospital grounds. Dr Wilkie had another visitor in his study, who was quickly dismissed as Sir William was announced.

'Thank you for coming forward and speaking up, MacIntyre,' the RMO told the youth meaningfully. 'I'll have a word with your Dean.'

'Thank you, sir.' The student, recognising Sheila, blushed and made his escape.

'Now, my dear fellow,' Sir William said heartily, 'I know you'll say I shouldn't

247

interfere in internal hospital business, but what's all this about Mark Leighton rifling my drug cupboard? He's left it rather late to start seeing that he's due to leave my firm in two weeks and is going to need a testimonial from me if he goes anywhere else. If the man's as daft as that I hope you have him in the psychiatric wing under restraint? By the way, this is—er—Doctor—Doctor—dammit, do I know your name, my dear?'

'Dr Devaney and I are already acquainted,' the RMO nodded smilingly at Sheila. 'Mr Leighton isn't under any restraint, Sir William, he's quite free to come and go as he pleases. In any case he is on leave until this evening.'

'Well, Dr Devaney and I are in the Mark Leighton Supporters' Club, and I thought you'd like to know that. Even before you have your hospital enquiry I would like to say that I will give him a job anytime, whatever your findings. I trust the boy implicitly.'

'I'm very glad to hear it, Sir William. Your opinion is valuable in the extreme. The young man who left as you arrived rather bears you out, too. He was the one who said originally that Mr Leighton had sold him the drugs he took. Now, in view of the later development, he has retracted his statement and admitted it was all lies. He took the keys when they were left unattended for a moment, and as Mr Leighton and Dr Devaney were both out of the hospital attending an emergency, they can neither of them be called to account for this laxness. Having rifled the cupboard and getting himself found out as a drug-taker, he then sought to have everybody blamed but himself. Fortunately for him he is a clever young man who used stimulants to increase his capacity for learning and sedatives to make himself sleep only as long as convenient. He has now learnt the error of his ways and will probably be severely censured and fined and allowed to carry on with his studies. As Mr Leighton's second supposed offence occurred so shortly after the first, each gave more credence to the other. Now that he is cleared of the first, however ...' There was a tap at the door and the RMO paused to call, 'Enter, please!'

Martha Haley came into the room glancing questioningly at Sir William and trying not to notice Sheila at all. She looked uncertain and decidedly on edge.

'My dear,' the consultant turned to Sheila and patted her hand, 'I wonder if you would run along and tell the RSO that I will be a little delayed? He will be in the senior residents' room, no doubt champing at the bit.' He patted the packet of manuscript.

'We'll keep this between ourselves for the time being, shall we? There may be no need ...' He winked significantly and Sheila gladly made her escape, somehow believing that Sir William knew exactly what he was doing.

After delivering the message to the Resident Surgical Officer, Sheila felt that she could manage Sunday lunch, which was usually quite edible compared with some mid-week meals, and it was after the steak pudding, while she was eating cherry pie with cream, that she was asked to attend once more upon the RMO. This time she came away smiling openly.

*   *   *

It seemed far longer than twenty-four hours since she had previously set foot on the *Lady Verity*. As she jumped down to the deck—the river was a little lower today—Mark popped his head out of the cabin.

'Thinking of angels—' he said, and took her openly into his arms. She was content to stay cheek to cheek for a few moments, for Mark had made this gesture without hearing her news. As he led her into the cabin he made others.

'Sheila,' he said seriously, 'I'm glad you've come because I was about to seek you out. We simply had to talk. I've been doing some very serious thinking about my future, but I can't think you out of it. It would be like trying to visualise daylight without the sun. Everything at the moment points to the fact that I'm not going to have a job for long, which will teach me to moan because I'm not allowed to emigrate! That seems small change now that I really have troubles. If these accusations against me stick then I may be struck off the rolls for a while. If I'd done what they say I would deserve to be. But proving I wasn't involved is going to be the very dickens because I've been well and truly framed by two separate parties. What I want to say, Sheila, is that I'll keep myself afloat somehow; not doing illegal abortions or anything like that, so don't worry; and when I reapply, having behaved myself, then I may get back straight away with a bit of luck. Could I ask— would it be audacious to ask—that in the circumstances you wait for me? The very minute all this blows over we'll be married. Of course I'll understand if you'd rather feel free in the meanwhile—I'll still come back and see you. I—I love you, Sheila. That's the only fact that's really meant anything all day. The rest is like a bad dream.'

There were twin stars in her eyes as she looked up at him.

'You mean that about marrying me the minute the unpleasantness blows over, Mark?'

'Of course I do.'

'Well, I may be able to manage one day next week if I rush. You see, it *has* blown over.'

He looked amazed, took her hands and tried to read the truth in her eyes.

'It's true, Mark. Sir William was your advocate all along. He told the RMO he'd give you a job no matter what conclusions the disciplinary committee came to. He and I really put our heads together with the result that Miss Haley admitted her part in the plot, and gave her reasons, and that student had already been shamed into owning up to the part he played. Sir William now wants you to take over Alpha and Beta Wards as Acting Registrar, and Martha is being asked to take leave, though Sir William says he wants her to come and see him afterwards. I think he'll offer her a job in his private clinic if she has really learnt her lesson. But the main thing is that you're cleared, and they let me come and tell you because I think they pretty well know how things are with us by now. You're to receive an official apology, etcetera. And in case in telling you all this I haven't mentioned it, Mark, I love you, too.'

She looked at him with heaven in her eyes and he felt that if he touched her at that

252

moment there would be no waiting for wedding bells, so he held himself in disciplinary bands of steel and closed his eyes.

'Let's ask our mamas if they're free next Thursday,' he suggested, at length. 'The hospital can keep its apologies and give my wife a week off instead. Does that appeal to you?'

The idea appealed to her so much that she felt dizzy for a moment and sought sanity anywhere she could. She tapped the envelope containing the thesis.

'You and I have to go through this together. It's been in alien hands since you saw it last. When it's typed and safely away about its business I can go on honeymoon, but not before. Are you ready to go to work?'

He said, battening down his happiness, 'Not really, but I'll make a supreme effort if you sit very close and hold my hand.'

Photoset, printed and bound in Great Britain by
REDWOOD BURN LIMITED, Trowbridge, Wiltshire